Words of Praise for

SPECIAL EDITION

from *New York Times* and *USA TODAY* bestselling authors

"When I started writing for Special Edition,
I was delighted by the length of the books,
which allowed the freedom to create,
and develop more within each character and
their romance. I have always been a fan of
Special Edition! I hope to write for it for many years
to come. Long live Special Edition!
—Diana Palmer

"My career began in Special Edition.
I remember my excitement when the SEs
were introduced, because the stories were so rich and
different, and every month when the books came out
I beat a path to the bookstore to get every one of them.
Here's to you, SE; live long, and prosper!"
—Linda Howard

"Congratulations, Special Edition,
on thirty years of publishing first-class romance!"
—Linda Lael Miller

"I owe a great deal to the Special Edition line for allowing me to grow as a writer. Special Edition did that, not only for me but for countless other authors over the past thirty years. It continues to offer compelling stories, with heroes and heroines readers love—and authors they've come to trust."
—Debbie Macomber

"Special Edition books always touch my heart. They are wonderful stories with the perfect happy ending."
—Susan Mallery

"How could I not love a series devoted to my favorite things—complex families and deep friendships? I'm so proud to have been a part of this wonderful tradition at Special Edition."
—Sherryl Woods

A COLD CREEK REUNION

RAEANNE THAYNE

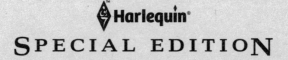

Harlequin®

SPECIAL EDITION

ISBN-13: 978-0-373-65661-5

A COLD CREEK REUNION

Copyright © 2012 by RaeAnne Thayne

THE ANNIVERSARY PARTY
Copyright © 2012 by Harlequin Books S.A.

Recycling programs
for this product may
not exist in your area.

The publisher acknowledges the following writers who contributed to THE ANNIVERSARY PARTY: RaeAnne Thayne, Christine Rimmer, Susan Crosby, Christyne Butler, Gina Wilkins and Cindy Kirk.

This edition published by arrangement with Harlequin Books S.A.

For questions and comments about the quality of this book please contact us at Customer_eCare@Harlequin.ca.

www.Harlequin.com

Printed in U.S.A.

CONTENTS

RAEANNE THAYNE

finds inspiration in the beautiful northern Utah mountains, where she lives with her husband and three children. Her books have won numerous honors, including RITA® Award nominations from Romance Writers of America and a Career Achievement Award from *RT Book Reviews*. RaeAnne loves to hear from readers and can be contacted through her website, www.raeannethayne.com.

Dear Reader,

I've read romance novels almost as long as I can remember. I think I picked up my first Harlequin romance when I was about eleven, and I instantly fell in love. I still love that thrill in my heart as I read about two people who deserve to find happiness together!

As I grew older, I discovered a whole new world of books out there and many fantastic authors whose stories have enriched my life more than I can say.

Here's a little secret for you. Though I've written for other romance lines over the years, Harlequin Special Edition has always been my favorite (and I'm not just saying that because I write for them now!). It was the very first line I ever submitted a manuscript to. Even twenty years ago when I started on this writing journey, I loved the stories about family, about home, about people learning how to entwine their lives together despite the challenges tugging them apart.

Once in a while I still have to pinch myself when I realize I'm actually writing for Special Edition now, the line that has given me so many wonderful hours of reading enjoyment over the years.

Happy anniversary, Special Edition. Here's to another wonderful thirty years!

RaeAnne Thayne

To romance readers who, like me,
love happily ever afters.

A COLD CREEK REUNION

Chapter One

He loved these guys like his own brothers, but some-times Taft Bowman wanted to take a fire hose to his whole blasted volunteer fire department.

This was their second swift-water rescue training in a month—not to mention that he had been holding these regularly since he became battalion chief five years earlier—and they still struggled to toss a throw bag anywhere close to one of the three "victims" float-ing down Cold Creek in wet suits and helmets.

"You've got to keep in mind the flow of the water and toss it downstream enough that they ride the current to the rope," he instructed for about the six-hundredth time. One by one, the floaters—in real-ity, other volunteer firefighters on his thirty-person crew—stopped at the catch line strung across the creek and began working their way hand over hand to the bank.

Fortunately, even though the waters were plenty frigid this time of year, they were about a month away from the real intensity of spring runoff, which was why he was training his firefighters for water rescues now.

With its twists and turns and spectacular surroundings on the west slope of the Tetons, Cold Creek had started gaining popularity with kayakers. He enjoyed floating the river himself. But between the sometimes-inexperienced outdoor-fun seekers and the occasional Pine Gulch citizen who strayed too close to the edge of the fast-moving water, his department was called out on at least a handful of rescues each season and he wanted them to be ready.

"Okay, let's try it one more time. Terry, Charlie, Bates, you three take turns with the throw bag. Luke, Cody, Tom, stagger your jumps by about five minutes this time around to give us enough time on this end to rescue whoever is ahead of you."

He set the team in position and watched upstream as Luke Orosco, his second in command, took a running leap into the water, angling his body feetfirst into the current. "Okay, Terry. He's coming. Are you ready? Time it just right. One, two, three. Now!"

This time, the rope sailed into the water just downstream of the diver and Taft grinned. "That's it, that's it. Perfect. Now instruct him to attach the rope."

For once, the rescue went smoothly. He was watching for Cody Shepherd to jump in when the radio clipped to his belt suddenly crackled with static.

"Chief Bowman, copy."

The dispatcher sounded unusually flustered and Taft's instincts borne of fifteen years of firefighting and paramedic work instantly kicked in. "Yeah, I copy. What's up, Kelly?"

"I've got a report of a small structure fire at the inn, three hundred twenty Cold Creek Road."

He stared as the second rescue went off without a hitch. "Come again?" he couldn't help asking, adrenaline pulsing through him. Structure fires were a rarity in the quiet town of Pine Gulch. Really a rarity. The last time had been a creosote chimney fire four months ago that a single ladder-truck unit had put out in about five minutes.

"Yes, sir. The hotel is evacuating at this time."

He muttered an oath. Half his crew was currently in wet suits, but at least they were only a few hundred yards away from the station house, with the engines and the turnout gear.

"Shut it down," he roared through his megaphone. "We've got a structure fire at the Cold Creek Inn. Grab your gear. This is not a drill."

To their credit, his crew immediately caught the gravity of the situation. The last floater was quickly grabbed out of the water and everybody else rushed to the new fire station the town had finally voted to bond for two years earlier.

Less than four minutes later—still too long in his book but not bad for volunteers—he had a full crew headed toward the Cold Creek Inn on a ladder truck and more trained volunteers pouring in to hurriedly don their turnout gear.

The inn, a rambling wood structure with two single-story wings leading off a main two-story building, was on the edge of Pine Gulch's small downtown, about a mile away from the station. He quickly assessed the situation as they approached. He couldn't see flames yet, but he did see a thin plume of black smoke coming from a window on the far end of the building's east wing.

He noted a few guests milling around on the lawn and had just an instant to feel a pang of sympathy for the owner. Poor Mrs. Pendleton had enough trouble finding guests for her gracefully historic but undeniably run-down inn.

A fire and forced evacuation probably wouldn't do much to increase the appeal of the place.

"Luke, you take Pete and make sure everybody's out. Shep, come with me for the assessment. You all know the drill."

He and Cody Shepherd, a young guy in the last stages of his fire and paramedic training, headed into the door closest to where he had seen the smoke.

Somebody had already been in here with a fire extinguisher, he saw. The fire was mostly out but the charred curtains were still smoking, sending out that inky-black plume.

The room looked to be under renovation. It didn't have a bed and the carpet had been pulled up. Everything was wet and he realized the ancient sprinkler system must have come on and finished the job the fire extinguisher had started.

"Is that it?" Shep asked with a disgruntled look.

"Sorry, should have let you have the honors." He

held the fire extinguisher out to the trainee. "Want a turn?"

Shep snorted but grabbed the fire extinguisher and sprayed another layer of completely unnecessary foam on the curtains.

"Not much excitement—but at least nobody was hurt. It's a wonder this place didn't go up years ago. We'll have to get the curtains out of here and have Engine Twenty come inside and check for hot spots."

He called in over his radio that the fire had been contained to one room and ordered in the team whose specialty was making sure the flames hadn't traveled inside the walls to silently spread to other rooms.

When he walked back outside, Luke headed over to him. "Not much going on, huh? Guess some of us should have stayed in the water."

"We'll do more swift-water work next week during training," he said. "Everybody else but Engine Twenty can go back to the station."

As he spoke to Luke, he spotted Jan Pendleton standing some distance away from the building. Even from here, he could see the distress on her plump, wrinkled features. She was holding a little dark-haired girl in her arms, probably a traumatized guest. Poor thing.

A younger woman stood beside her and from this distance he had only a strange impression, as if she was somehow standing on an island of calm amid the chaos of the scene, the flashing lights of the emergency vehicles, shouts between his crew members, the excited buzz of the crowd.

And then the woman turned and he just about

tripped over a snaking fire hose somebody shouldn't have left there.

Laura.

He froze and for the first time in fifteen years as a firefighter, he forgot about the incident, his mission, just what the hell he was doing here.

Laura.

Ten years. He hadn't seen her in all that time, since the week before their wedding when she had given him back his ring and left town. Not just town. She had left the whole damn country, as if she couldn't run far enough to get away from him.

Some part of him desperately wanted to think he had made some kind of mistake. It couldn't be her. That was just some other slender woman with a long sweep of honey-blond hair and big blue, unforgettable eyes. But no, it was definitely Laura, standing next to her mother. Sweet and lovely.

Not his.

"Chief, we're not finding any hot spots." Luke approached him. Just like somebody turned back up the volume on his flat-screen, he jerked away from memories of pain and loss and aching regret.

"You're certain?"

"So far. The sprinkler system took a while to kick in and somebody with a fire extinguisher took care of the rest. Tom and Nate are still checking the integrity of the internal walls."

"Good. That's good. Excellent work."

His assistant chief gave him a wary look. "You okay, Chief? You look upset."

He huffed out a breath. "It's a fire, Luke. It could

have been potentially disastrous. With the ancient wiring in this old building, it's a wonder the whole thing didn't go up."

"I was thinking the same thing," Luke said.

He was going to have to go over there and talk to Mrs. Pendleton—and by default, Laura. He didn't want to. He wanted to stand here and pretend he hadn't seen her. But he was the fire chief. He couldn't hide out just because he had a painful history with the daughter of the property owner.

Sometimes he hated his job.

He made his way toward the women, grimly aware of his heart pounding in his chest as if he had been the one diving into Cold Creek for training.

Laura stiffened as he approached but she didn't meet his gaze. Her mother looked at him out of wide, frightened eyes and her arms tightened around the girl in her arms.

Despite everything, his most important job was calming her fears. "Mrs. Pendleton, you'll be happy to know the fire is under control."

"Of course it's under control." Laura finally faced him, her lovely features cool and impassive. "It was under control before your trucks ever showed up—ten minutes after we called the fire in, by the way."

Despite all the things he might have wanted to say to her, he had to first bristle at any implication that their response time might be less than adequate. "Seven, by my calculations. Would have been half that except we were in the middle of water rescue training when the call from dispatch came in."

"I guess you would have been ready, then, if any

of our guests had decided to jump into Cold Creek to avoid the flames."

Funny, he didn't remember her being this tart when they had been engaged. He remembered sweetness and joy and light. Until he had destroyed all that.

"Chief Bowman, when will we be able to allow our guests to return to their rooms?" Jan Pendleton spoke up, her voice wobbling a little. The little girl in her arms—who shared Laura's eye color, he realized now, along with the distinctive features of someone born with Down syndrome—patted her cheek.

"Gram, don't cry."

Jan visibly collected herself and gave the girl a tired smile.

"They can return to get their belongings as long as they're not staying in the rooms adjacent to where the fire started. I'll have my guys stick around about an hour or so to keep an eye on some hot spots." He paused, wishing he didn't have to be the bearer of this particular bad news. "I'm going to leave the final decision up to you about your guests staying here overnight, but to be honest, I'm not sure it's completely safe for guests to stay here tonight. No matter how careful we are, sometimes embers can flare up again hours later."

"We have a dozen guests right now." Laura looked at him directly and he was almost sure he saw a hint of hostility there. Annoyance crawled under his skin. *She* dumped him, a week before their wedding. If anybody here had the right to be hostile, he ought to be the first one in line. "What are we supposed to do with them?"

Their past didn't matter right now, not when people

in his town needed his help. "We can talk to the Red Cross about setting up a shelter, or we can check with some of the other lodgings in town, maybe the Cavazos' guest cabins, and see if they might have room to take a few."

Mrs. Pendleton closed her eyes. "This is a disaster."

"But a fixable one, Mom. We'll figure something out." She squeezed her mother's arm.

"Any idea what might have started the fire?" He had to ask.

Laura frowned and something that looked oddly like guilt shifted across her lovely features. "Not the *what* exactly, but most likely the *who*."

"Oh?"

"Alexandro Santiago. Come here, young man."

He followed her gaze and for the first time, he noticed a young dark-haired boy of about six or seven sitting on the curb, watching the activity at the scene with a sort of avid fascination in his huge dark brown eyes. The boy didn't have her blond, blue-eyed coloring, but he shared her wide, mobile mouth, slender nose and high cheekbones, and was undoubtedly her child.

The kid didn't budge from the curb for a long, drawn-out moment, but he finally rose slowly to his feet and headed toward them as if he were on his way to bury his dog in the backyard.

"Alex, tell the fireman what started the fire."

The boy shifted his stance, avoiding the gazes of both his mother and Taft. "Do I have to?"

"Yes," Laura said sternly.

The kid fidgeted a little more and finally sighed.

"Okay. I found a lighter in one of the empty rooms. The ones being fixed up." He spoke with a very slight, barely discernible accent. "I never saw one before and I only wanted to see how it worked. I didn't mean to start a fire, *es la verdad.* But the curtains caught fire and I yelled and then *mi madre* came in with the fire extinguisher."

Under other circumstances he might have been amused at the no-nonsense way the kid told the story and how he manipulated events to make it seem as if everything had just sort of happened without any direct involvement on his part.

But this could have been a potentially serious situation, a crumbling old fire hazard like the inn.

He hated to come off hard-nosed and mean, but he had to make the kid understand the gravity. Education was a huge part of his job and a responsibility he took very seriously. "That was a very dangerous thing to do. People could have been seriously hurt. If your mother hadn't been able to get to the room fast enough with the fire extinguisher, the flames could have spread from room to room and burned down the whole hotel and everything in it."

To his credit, the boy met his gaze. Embarrassment and shame warred on his features. "I know. It was stupid. I'm really, really sorry."

"The worst part of it is, I have told you again and again not to play with matches or lighters or anything else that can cause a fire. We've talked about the dangers." Laura glowered at her son, who squirmed.

"I just wanted to see how it worked," he said, his voice small.

"You won't do it again, will you?" Taft said.

"Never. Never, ever."

"Good, because we're pretty strict about this kind of thing around here. Next time you'll have to go to jail."

The boy gave him a wide-eyed look, but then sighed with relief when he noticed Taft's half grin. "I won't do it again, I swear. Pinky promise."

"Excellent."

"Hey, Chief," Lee Randall called from the engine. "We're having a little trouble with the hose retractor again. Can you give us a hand?"

"Yeah. Be there in a sec," he called back, grateful for any excuse to escape the awkwardness of seeing her again.

"Excuse me, won't you?" he said to the Pendleton women and the children.

"Of course." Jan Pendleton gave him an earnest look. "Please tell your firefighters how very much we appreciate them, don't we, Laura?"

"Absolutely," she answered with a dutiful tone, but he noticed she pointedly avoided meeting his gaze.

"Bye, Chief." The darling little girl in Jan's arm gave him a generous smile. Oh, she was a charmer, he thought.

"See you later."

The girl beamed at him and waved as he headed away, feeling as if somebody had wrapped a fire hose around his neck for the past ten minutes.

She was here. Really here. Blue eyes, cute kids and all.

Laura Pendleton, Santiago now. He had loved her

with every bit of his young heart and she had walked away from him without a second glance.

Now she was here and he had no way to avoid her, not living in a small town like Pine Gulch that had only one grocery store, a couple of gas stations and a fire station only a few blocks from her family's hotel.

He was swamped with memories suddenly, memories he didn't want and didn't know what to do with.

She was back. And here he had been thinking lately how lucky he was to be fire chief of a small town with only six thousand people that rarely saw any disasters.

Taft Bowman.

Laura watched him head back into the action—which, really, wasn't much action at all, given that the fire had been extinguished before any of them arrived. He paused here and there in the parking lot to talk to his crew, snap out orders, adjust some kind of mechanical thing on the sleek red fire truck.

Seeing him in action was nothing new. When they had been dating, she sometimes went on ride-alongs, mostly because she couldn't bear to be separated from him. She remembered now how Taft had always seemed comfortable and in control of any situation, whether responding to a medical emergency or dealing with a grass fire.

Apparently that hadn't changed in the decade since she had seen him. He also still had that very sexy, lean-hipped walk, even under the layers of turnout gear. She watched him for just a moment, then forced herself to look away. This little tingle of remembered desire inside her was wrong on so many levels, completely twisted and messed up.

After all these years and all the pain, all those shards of crushed dreams she finally had to sweep up and throw away, how could he still have the power to affect her at all? She should be cool and impervious to him, completely untouched.

When she finally made the decision to come home after Javier's death, she had known she would inevitably run into Taft. Pine Gulch was a small town after all. No matter how much a person might wish to, it was generally tough to avoid someone forever.

When she thought about it—and she would be lying to herself if she said she *hadn't* thought about it—she had foolishly imagined she could greet him with only a polite smile and a *Nice to see you again,* remaining completely impervious to the man.

Their shared history was a long time ago. Another lifetime, it seemed. She had made the only possible choice back then and had completely moved on with her life, had married someone else, given birth to two children and put Pine Gulch far in her past.

As much as she had loved him once, Taft was really just a small chapter in her life. Or so she told herself anyway. She had been naively certain she had dealt with the hurt and betrayal and the deep sense of loss long ago.

Maybe she should have put a little more energy and effort into making certain of all that before she packed up her children and moved thousands of miles from the only home they had ever known.

If she'd had a little energy to spare, she might have

given it more thought, but the past six months seemed like a whirlwind, first trying to deal with Javier's estate and the vast debts he had left behind, then that desperate scramble to juggle her dwindling bank account and two hungry children in expensive Madrid, and finally the grim realization that she couldn't do it by herself and had no choice but to move her little family across the world and back to her mother.

She had been focused on survival, on doing what she thought was right for her children. She supposed she really hadn't wanted to face the reality that moving back also meant dealing with Taft again—until it smacked her upside the head, thanks to her rascal of a son and his predilection for finding trouble wherever he could.

"What are we going to do?" Her mother fretted beside her. She set Maya down on the concrete sidewalk, and the girl immediately scampered beside Alex and stood holding her brother's hand while they watched the firefighters now cleaning up the scene and driving away. "This is going to ruin us!"

Laura put an arm around her mother's plump shoulders, guilt slicing through her. She should have been watching her son more carefully; she certainly knew better than to give him any free rein. She had allowed herself to become distracted checking in some guests—the young married couple on spring break from graduate school in Washington who had found more excitement than they had probably anticipated when their hotel caught fire before they had even seen their room.

While she was busy with them, Alex must have

slipped out of the office and wandered to the wing of the hotel they were currently renovating. She still couldn't believe he had found a lighter somewhere. Maybe a previous guest had left it or one of the subcontractors who had been coming in and out the past week or so.

It really *was* a miracle her son hadn't been injured or burned the whole place down.

"You heard Chief Bowman. The fire and smoke damage was contained to only one room, so that's good news."

"How is any of this good news?" In the flash of the emergency vehicles as they pulled away, her mother's features looked older somehow and her hands shook as she pushed a stray lock of carefully colored hair away.

Despite Taft and all the memories that had suddenly been dredged up simply by exchanging a few words with the man, she didn't regret coming back to Pine Gulch. The irony was, she thought she was coming home because she needed her mother's help only to discover how very much Jan needed hers.

Care and upkeep on this crumbling twenty-room inn were obviously wearing on her mother. Jan had been deeply grateful to turn some of those responsibilities over to her only daughter.

"It could be much worse, Mom. We have to focus on that. No one was hurt. That's the important thing. And outdated as it is, the sprinkler system worked better than we might have expected. That's another plus. Besides, look at it this way—now insurance will cover some of the repairs we already planned."

"I suppose. But what are we going to do with the

guests?" Her mother seemed defeated, overwhelmed, all but wringing her hands.

Laura hugged her again. "Don't worry about anything. In fact, why don't you take the children back to the house? I think they've had enough excitement for one afternoon."

"Do you think Chief Bowman will consider it safe?"

Laura glanced over at the three-bedroom cottage behind the inn where she had spent her childhood. "It's far enough from the action. I can't see why it would be a problem. Meantime, I'll start making phone calls. We'll find places for everyone and for our reservations for the next few nights while the smoke damage clears out. We'll get through this just like everything else."

"I'm so glad you're here, my dear. I don't know what I would do without you."

If she *hadn't* been here—along with her daughter and her little firebug of a son—none of this would have happened.

"So am I, Mom," she answered. It was the truth, despite having to confront a certain very sexy fire chief with whom she shared a tangled history.

"Oh, I should go talk to poor Mr. Baktiri. He probably doesn't quite understand what's going on."

One of their long-term guests stood in the middle of the lawn, looking at the hectic scene with confusion. She remembered Mr. Baktiri from when she was a girl. He and his wife used to run the drive-in on the outskirts of town. Mrs. Baktiri had passed away and Mr. Baktiri had moved with his son to Idaho Falls, but he apparently hated it there. Once a month or so, he would escape back to Pine Gulch to visit his wife's graveside.

Her mother gave him substantially reduced rates on their smallest room, where he stayed for a week or two at a time until his son would come down from Idaho Falls to take him back home. It wasn't a very economically feasible operating procedure, but she couldn't fault her mother for her kindness.

She had the impression Mr. Baktiri might be suffering from mild dementia and she supposed familiar surroundings were a comfort to him.

"Mommy. Lights." Maya hugged her legs and looked up, the flashing emergency lights reflecting in her thick glasses.

"I know, sweetie. They're bright, aren't they?"

"Pretty."

"I suppose they are, in a way."

Trust Maya to find joy in any situation. It was her child's particular skill and she was deeply grateful for it.

She had a million things to do, most pressing to find somewhere for their guests to spend the night, but for now she gathered this precious child in her arms.

Out of the corner of her gaze, she saw Alex edge toward them somewhat warily.

"Come here, *niño,*" she murmured.

He sank into her embrace and she held both children close. This was the important thing. As she had told her mother, they would get through this minor setback. She was a survivor. She had survived a broken

Chapter Two

"Guess who I saw in town the other day."

Taft grabbed one of his sister's delicious dinner rolls from the basket being passed around his family's dining-room table and winked at Caidy. "Me, doing something awesome and heroic, probably. Fighting a fire. Saving someone's life. I don't know. Could be anything."

His niece, Destry, and Gabrielle Parsons, whose older sister was marrying Taft's twin brother, Trace, in a few months, both giggled—just as he had intended—but Caidy only rolled her eyes. "News flash. Not everything is about you, Taft. But oddly, in a way, this is."

"Who did you see?" he asked, though he was aware of a glimmer of uneasy trepidation, already expecting what was coming next.

"I didn't have a chance to talk to her. I just happened to see her while I was driving," Caidy said.

"Who?" he asked again, teetering on the brink of annoyance.

"Laura Pendleton," Caidy announced.

"Not Pendleton anymore," Ridge, their older brother and Destry's father, corrected.

"That's right," Trace chimed in from the other side of the table, where he was holding hands with Becca. How the heck did they manage to eat when they couldn't seem to keep their hands off each other? Taft wondered.

"She got married to some guy while she was living in Spain and they had a couple of kids," Trace went on. "I hear one of them was involved in all the excitement the other day at the inn."

Taft pictured her kid solemnly promising he wouldn't play with matches again. He'd picked up the definite vibe that the kid was a mischievous little rascal, but for all that, his sincerity had rung true.

"Yeah. Apparently her older kid, Alex, was a little too curious about a lighter he found in an empty room and caught some curtains on fire."

"And you had to ride to her rescue?" Caidy gave him a wide-eyed look. "Gosh, that must have been awkward for both of you."

Taft reached for more mashed potatoes, hoping the heat on his face could be attributed to the steaming bowl.

"Why would it be? Everything was fine," he muttered.

Okay, that was a lie, but his family didn't necessarily need to know he hadn't been able to stop thinking about Laura for the past few days. Every time he had a quiet moment, her blue eyes and delicate features would pop into his head and some other half-forgotten memory of their time together would emerge like the Tetons rising out of a low fog bank.

That he couldn't seem to stop them annoyed him. He had worked damn hard to forget her after she walked away. What was he supposed to do now that she was back in town and he couldn't escape her or her kids or the weight of all his mistakes?

"You'll have to catch me up here." Becca, Trace's fiancée, looked confused as she reached for her glass. "Who's Laura Pendleton? I'm taking a wild guess here that she must be related to Mrs. Pendleton at the inn somehow—a client of mine, by the way—but why would it be awkward to have Taft put out a fire at the inn?"

"No reason really." Caidy flashed him a quick look. "Just that Taft and Laura were engaged once."

He fidgeted with his mashed potatoes, drawing his fork in a neat little firebreak to keep the gravy from spreading while he avoided the collective gaze of his beloved family. Why, again, had he once enjoyed these Sunday dinners?

"Engaged? Taft?" He didn't need to look at his future sister-in-law to hear the surprise in her voice.

"I know," his twin brother said. "Hard to believe, right?"

He looked up just in time to see Becca quickly try to hide her shocked gaze. She was too kindhearted to let him see how stunning she found the news, which somehow bothered him even more.

Okay, maybe he had a bit of a reputation in town—most of it greatly exaggerated—as a bit of a player. Becca knew him by now. She should know how silly it all was.

"When was this?" she asked with interest. "Recently?"

"Years ago," Ridge said. "He and Laura dated just out of high school—"

"College," he muttered. "She was in college." Okay, she had been a freshman in college. But she wasn't in high school, damn it. That point seemed important somehow.

"They were inseparable," Trace interjected.

Ridge picked up where he'd left off. "And Taft proposed right around the time Laura graduated from the Montana State."

"What happened?" Becca asked.

He really didn't want to talk about this. What he wouldn't give for a good emergency call right now. Nothing big. No serious personal injury or major property damage. How about a shed fire or a kid stuck in a well or something?

"We called things off."

"The week before the wedding," Caidy added.

Oh, yes. Don't forget to add that little salacious detail.

"It was a mutual decision," he lied, repeating the blatant fiction that Laura had begged him to uphold. Mutual decision. Right. If by *mutual* he meant *Laura* and if by *decision* he meant *crush-the-life-out-of-a-guy blow.*

Laura had dumped him. That was the cold, hard truth. A week before their wedding, after all the plans and deposits and dress fittings, she had given him back his ring and told him she couldn't marry him.

"Why are we talking about ancient history?" he asked.

"Not so ancient anymore," Trace said. "Not if Laura's back in town."

He was very much afraid his brother was right. Whether he liked it or not, with her once more residing in Pine Gulch, their past together would be dredged up again—and not by just his family.

Questions would swirl around them. Everybody had to remember that they had been just a few days away from walking down the aisle of the little church in town when things ended and Laura and her mother sent out those regrets and made phone calls announcing the big celebration wasn't happening—while he had gone down to the Bandito and gotten drunk and stayed that way until about a month or two after the wedding day that didn't happen.

She was back now, which meant that, like it or not, he would have to deal with everything he had shoved down ten years ago, all the emotions he had pretended weren't important in order to get through the deep, aching loss of her.

He couldn't blame his family for their curiosity—not even Trace, his twin and best friend, knew the full story about everything that had happened between him and Laura. He had always considered it his private business.

His family had loved her. Who didn't? Laura had a knack for drawing people toward her, finding commonalities. She and his mother used to love discussing the art world and painting techniques. His mother had been an artist, only becoming renowned around the time of her murder. While Laura hadn't any particular skill in that direction, she had shared a genuine appreciation for his parents' extensive art collection.

His father had adored her, too, and had often told Taft that Laura was the best thing that would ever happen to him.

He looked up from the memory to find Becca's eyes filled with a compassion that made him squirm and lose whatever appetite he might have had left.

"I'm sorry," she murmured in that kind way she had. "Mutual decision or not, it still must have been painful. Is it hard for you to see her again?"

He faked a nonchalant look. "Hard? Why would it be hard? It was all a decade ago. She's moved on. I've moved on. No big deal."

Ridge gave what sounded like a fake cough and Trace had the same skeptical expression on his face he always wore when Taft was trying to talk him into living a little, doing something wild and adventurous for a change.

How was it possible to love his siblings and at the same time want to throw a few punches around the table, just on general principles?

Becca eyed him and then his brothers warily as if

sensing his discomfort, then she quickly changed the subject. "How's the house coming?" she asked.

His brother wasn't nearly good enough for her, he decided, seizing the diversion. "Good. I've got only a couple more rooms to drywall. Should be done soon. After six months, the place is starting to look like a real house inside now."

"I stopped by the other day and peeked in the windows," Caidy confessed. "It's looking great."

"Give me a call next time and I can swing by and give you the tour, even if I'm at the fire station. You haven't been by in a month or so. You'll be surprised at how far along it is these days."

After years of renting a convenient but small apartment near the fire station, he had finally decided it was time to build a real house. The two-story log house was set on five acres near the mouth of Cold Creek Canyon.

"How about the barn and the pasture?" Ridge asked, rather predictably. Over the years, Taft had bred a couple mares to a stallion with excellent lines he had picked up for a steal from a rancher down on his luck up near Wood River. He had traded and sold the colts until he now had about six horses he'd been keeping at his family's ranch.

"The fence is in. I'd like to get the barn up before I move the horses over, if you don't mind keeping them a little longer."

"That's not what I meant. You know we've got plenty of room here. You can keep them here forever if you want."

Maybe if he had his horses closer he might actually

ride them once in a while instead of only stopping by to visit when he came for these Sunday dinners.

"When do you think all the work will be done?" Becca asked.

"I'm hoping by mid-May. Depends on how much free time I can find to finish things up inside."

"If you need a hand, let me know," Ridge offered quietly.

"Same goes," Trace added.

Both of them had crazy-busy lives: Ridge running the ranch and raising Destry on his own and Trace as the overworked chief of police for an understaffed small-town force—in addition to planning his future together with Becca and Gabi. Their sincere offers to help touched him.

"I should be okay," he answered. "The hard work is done now and I only have the fun stuff to finish."

"I always thought there was something just a little crazy about you." Caidy shook her head. "I must be right, especially if you think finish work and painting are fun."

"I like to paint stuff," Destry said. "I can help you, Uncle Taft."

"Me, too!" Gabrielle exclaimed. "Oh, can we?"

Trouble followed the two of these girls around like one of Caidy's rescue dogs. He had visions of paint spread all over the woodwork he had been slaving over the past month. "Thanks, girls. That's really sweet of you. I'm sure Ridge can find something for you to touch up around here. That fence down by the creek was looking like it needed a new coat."

"There's always something that needs painting

around here," Ridge answered. "As soon as the weather warms up a little at night, I can put you both to work."

"Will you pay us?" Gabrielle asked, always the opportunist.

Ridge chuckled. "We can negotiate terms with your attorney."

Caidy asked Becca—said attorney—a question about their upcoming June wedding and attention shifted away from Taft, much to his relief. He listened to the conversation of his family, aware of this low simmer of restlessness that had become a familiar companion.

Ever since Trace and Becca found each other and fell in love, he had been filled with this vague unease, as if something about his world had shifted a little. He loved his brother. More than that, he respected him. Trace was his best friend and Taft could never begrudge him the happiness he had found with Becca and Gabi, but ever since they announced their engagement, he felt weird and more than a little off-balance.

Seeing Laura and her kids the other day had only intensified that odd feeling.

He had never been a saint—he would be the first to admit that and his family would probably stand in line right behind him—but he tried to live a decent life. His general philosophy about the world ran parallel to the premier motto of every emergency medical worker as well as others in the medical field: Primum Non Nocere. First, Do No Harm.

He did his best. He was a firefighter and paramedic and he enjoyed helping people of his community and protecting property. If he didn't find great satisfaction in it, he would find something else to do. Maybe pounding nails for a living because he enjoyed that, too.

Despite his best efforts in the whole *do no harm* arena, he remembered each and every failure.

He had two big regrets in his life, and Laura Pendleton was involved in both of them.

He had hurt her. Those months leading up to her ultimate decision to break things off had been filled with one wound after another. He knew it. Hell, he had known it at the time, but that dark, angry man he had become after his parents' murder seemed like another creature who had emerged out of his skin to destroy everything good and right in his life.

He couldn't blame Laura for calling off their wedding. Not really. Even though it had hurt like the devil.

She had warned him she couldn't marry him unless he made serious changes, and he had stubbornly refused, giving her no choice but to stay true to her word. She had moved on, taken some exotic job in hotel management in Spain somewhere and a few years later married a man she met there.

The reminder of her marriage left him feeling petty and small. Yeah, he had hurt her, but his betrayal probably didn't hold a candle to everything else she had lost—her husband and the father of her children, whom he'd heard had drowned about six months earlier.

"Are you planning on eating any of that or just pushing it around your plate?"

He glanced up and, much to his shock, discovered Ridge was the only one left at the table. Everybody

—not that stress alone could explain her mother

ing such an incomprehensible decision.

Really, it was all your idea," Jan said calmly.

My idea?" Impossible. Even in her most tangled

tmare, she never would have come up with this

sible scenario.

Yes. Weren't you just saying the other day how

ch it would help to have a carpenter on the staff to

with the repairs, especially now that we totally

e to start from the ground up in the fire-damaged

m?"

"I say a lot of things, Mom." *That doesn't mean I*

nt you to rush out and enter into a deal with a par-

ular devil named Taft Bowman.

"I just thought you would appreciate the help, that's

. I know how much the fire has complicated your

neline for the renovation."

"Not really. Only one room was damaged and it was

eady on my schedule for renovations."

"Well, when Chief Bowman stopped by this morn-

to check on things after the excitement we had

other day—which I thought was a perfectly lovely

by the way—he mentioned he could lend us a

pairs in his free time. Honestly, dar-

perfect solution."

's ex-fiancé take an

else had cleared off while he had been lost in thought, and he hadn't even noticed.

"Sorry. Been a long couple of days." He hoped his brother didn't notice the heat he could feel crawling over his features.

Ridge gave him a long look and Taft sighed, waiting for the inevitable words of advice from his brother.

As the oldest Bowman sibling left after their parents died, Ridge had taken custody of Caidy, who had been a teenager at the time. Even though Taft and Trace had both been in their early twenties, Ridge still tried to take over the role of father figure to them, too, whether they liked it or not—which they usually didn't.

Instead of a lecture, Ridge only sipped at his drink. "I was thinking about taking the girls for a ride up to check the fence line on the high pasture. Want to come along? A little mountain air might help clear your head."

He did love being on the back of a horse amid the pine and sage of the mountains overlooking the ranch, but he wasn't in the mood for more questions or sympathy from his family about Laura.

"To tell you the truth, I'm itching to get my hands dirty. I think I'll head over to the house and put in a window frame or something."

Ridge nodded. "I know you've got plenty to do on your own place, but I figured this was worth mentioning, too. I heard the other day at the hardware store that Jan Pendleton is looking to hire somebody to help her with some renovations to the inn."

He snorted. As if Laura would ever let her mother

hire him. He figured Ridge was joking but he didn't see any hint of humor in his brother's expression.

"Just saying. I thought you might be interested in helping Laura and her mother out a little."

Ah. Without actually offering a lecture, this must be Ridge's way of reminding Taft he owed Laura something. None of the rest of the family knew what had happened all those years ago, but he was pretty sure all of them blamed him.

And they were right.

Without answering, he shoved away from the table and grabbed his plate to carry it into the kitchen. First, do no harm. But once the harm had been done, a stand-up guy found some way to make it right. No matter how difficult.

min
mak
"
"
nig
pos

mu
hel
ha
ro

wa
tic

al
ti

al

ing
the
ges

Chapter Three

Laura stared at her mother, shock buzzin
her as if she had just bent down and licked
cal outlet.

"Sorry, say that again. You did *what?*"

"I didn't think you'd mind, darling,"
said, with a vague sort of smile as she co
ring the chicken she was cooking for the

Are you completely mental? she wa
could you possibly think I would

She drew a deep

always agree with her mother's methods and might have run things differently if she had been home, Laura knew Jan had tried hard to keep the inn functioning all those years she had been living in Madrid.

But she still couldn't wrap her head around this one. "In theory, it is a good idea. A resident carpenter would come in very handy. But not Taft, for heaven's sake, Mom!"

Jan frowned in what appeared to be genuine confusion. "You mean because of your history together?"

"For a start. Seeing him again after all these years is more than a little awkward," she admitted.

Her mother continued to frown. "I'm sorry but I don't understand. What am I missing? You always insisted your breakup was a mutual decision. I distinctly remember you telling me over and over again you had both decided you were better off as friends."

Had she said that? She didn't remember much about that dark time other than her deep despair.

"You were so cool and calm after your engagement ended, making all those terrible phone calls, returning all those wedding presents. You acted like you didn't care at all. Honey, I honestly thought you wouldn't mind having Taft here now or I never would have taken him up on his suggestion."

Ah. Her lying little chickens were now com___ home to roost. Laura fought the urge to bang h___ on the old pine kitchen table a few doze___

Ten years ago, she had worked s___ everyone involved that nobody ___ tered by the implosion of their en___ ents, she had put on a bright, happy___ to be excited about the adventures awaiting her, knowing how crushed they would have been if they caught even a tiny glimmer of the truth—that inside her heart felt like a vast, empty wasteland.

How could she blame her mother for not seeing through her carefully constructed act to the stark and painful reality, especially when only a few years later, Laura was married to someone else and expecting Jan's first grandchild? It was unfair to be hurt, to wish Jan had somehow glimpsed the depth of her hidden heartache.

This, then, was her own fault. Well, hers and a certain opportunistic male who had always been very good at charming her mother—and every other female within a dozen miles of Pine Gulch.

"Okay, the carpentry work. I get that. Yes, we certainly need the help and Taft is very good with his hands." She refused to remember just *how* good those hands could be. "But did you have to offer him a room?"

Jan shrugged, adding a lemony sauce to the chicken that instantly started to burble, filling the kitchen with a delicious aroma. "That was his idea."

Oh, Laura was quite sure it *was* Taft's idea. The bigger question was *why?* What possible reason could he have for this sudden wish to stay at the inn? By the stunned look he had worn when he spotted her at the fire scene, she would have assumed he wanted to stay as far away from her as possible.

He had to find this whole situation as awkward and, yes, painful as she did.

Maybe it was all some twisted revenge plot. She had

spurned him after all. Maybe he wanted to somehow punish her all these years later with shoddy carpentry work that would end up costing an arm and a leg to repair....

She sighed at her own ridiculous imaginings. Taft didn't work that way. Whatever his motive for making this arrangement with her mother, she had no doubt he would put his best effort into the job.

"Apparently his lease was up on the apartment where he's been living," Jan went on. "He's building a house in Cold Creek Canyon—which I've heard is perfectly lovely, by the way—but it won't be finished for a few more weeks. Think of how much you can save on paying for a carpenter, all in exchange only for letting him stay in a room that was likely to be empty anyway, the way our vacancy rate will be during the shoulder season until the summer tourist activity heats up. I honestly thought you would be happy about this. When Taft suggested it, the whole thing seemed like a good solution all the way around."

A good solution for everyone except *her!* How would she survive having him underfoot all the time, smiling at her out of those green eyes she had once adored so much, talking to her out of that delicious mouth she had tasted many times?

She gave a tiny sigh and her mother sent her a careful look. "I can still tell him no. He was planning on bringing some of his things over in the morning, but I'll just give him a ring and tell him never mind. We can find someone else, honey, if having Taft here will make you too uncomfortable."

Her mother was completely sincere, she knew. Jan

would call him in immediately if she had any idea how much Laura had grieved for the dreams they had once spun together.

For an instant, she was tempted to have her mother do exactly that, call and tell him the deal was off.

How could she, though? She knew just what Taft would think. He would guess, quite accurately, that she was the one who didn't want him here and would know she had dissuaded her mother from the plan.

Her shoulder blades itched at the thought. She didn't want him thinking she was uncomfortable having him around. Better that he continue to believe she was completely indifferent to the ramifications of being back in Pine Gulch with him.

She had done her very best to strike the proper tone the day of the fire, polite but cool, as if they were distant acquaintances instead of once having shared everything.

If she told her mother she didn't want to have Taft here, he would know her demeanor was all an act.

She was trapped. Well and truly trussed, just like one of the calves he used to rope in the high-school rodeo. It was a helpless, miserable feeling, one that felt all too familiar. She had lived with it every day of the past seven years, since her marriage to Javier Santiago. But unlike those calves in the rodeo ring, she had wandered willingly into the ropes that bound her to a man she didn't love.

Well, she hadn't been completely willing, she supposed. From the beginning she had known marrying him was a mistake and had tried every way she could think short of jilting him also to escape the ties binding them together. But unlike with Taft, this time she'd had a third life to consider. She had been four months pregnant with Alexandro. Javier—strangely old-fashioned about this, at least—wouldn't consider any other option but marriage.

She had tried hard to convince herself she was in love with him. He was handsome and seductively charming and made her laugh with his extravagant pursuit of her, which had been the reason she had finally given in and begun to date him while she was working at the small, exclusive boutique hotel he owned in Madrid.

She had tried to be a good wife and had worked hard to convince herself she loved him, but it hadn't been enough. Not for him and not for her—but by then she had been thoroughly entangled in the piggin' rope, so to speak, by Alex and then by Maya, her sweet-natured and vulnerable daughter.

This, though, with Taft. She couldn't control what her mother had done, but she could certainly control her own response to it. She wouldn't allow herself to care if the man had suddenly invaded every inch of her personal space by moving into the hotel. It was only temporary and then he would be out of her life again.

"Do you want me to call him?" her mother asked again.

She forced herself to smile. "Not at all, Mama. I'm sorry. I was just…surprised, that's all. Everything should be fine. You're right—it's probably a great idea. Free labor is always a good thing, and like you said, the only thing we're giving up is a room that probably wouldn't have been booked anyway."

Maya wandered into the kitchen, apparently tired of playing, and gave her mother one of those generous hugs Laura had come to depend upon like oxygen and water. "Hungry, Mama."

"Gram is fixing us something delicious for dinner. Aren't we lucky to have her?"

Maya nodded with a broad smile to her grand-mother. "Love you, Gram."

"I love you, too, sweetheart." Jan beamed back at her.

This—her daughter and Alex—was more impor-tant than her discomfort about Taft. She was trying her best to turn the hotel into something that could actu-ally turn a profit instead of just provide a subsistence for her mother and now her and her children.

She had her chance to live her lifelong dream now and make the Cold Creek Inn into the warm and gra-cious facility she had always imagined, a place where families could feel comfortable to gather, where cou-ples could find or rekindle romance, where the occa-sional business traveler could find a home away from home.

This was her moment to seize control of her life and make a new future for herself and her children. She couldn't let Taft ruin that for her.

All she had to do was remind herself that she hadn't loved him for ten years and she should be able to handle his presence here at the inn with calm aplomb.

No big deal whatsoever. Right?

If some part of him had hoped Laura might fall all over him with gratitude for stepping up to help with the inn renovations, Taft would have been doomed to disappointment.

Over the next few days, as he settled into his surprisingly comfortable room in the wing overlooking the creek, a few doors down from the fire-damaged room, he helped Mrs. Pendleton with the occasional carpentry job. A bathroom cabinet repair here, a countertop fix there. In that time, he barely saw Laura. Somehow she was always mysteriously absent whenever he stopped at the front desk.

The few times he did come close enough to talk to her, she would exchange a quick, stiff word with him and then manufacture some excuse to take off at the earliest opportunity, as if she didn't want to risk some kind of contagion.

She had dumped *him,* not the other way around, but she was acting as if he was the biggest heel in the county. Still, he found her prickly, standoffish attitude more a challenge than an annoyance.

Truth was, he wasn't used to women ignoring him— and he certainly wasn't accustomed to *Laura* ignoring him.

They had been friends forever, even before that momentous summer after her freshman year of college when he finally woke up and realized how much he had come to care about her as much more than simply a friend. After she left, he had missed the woman he loved with a hollow ache he had never quite been able to fill, but he sometimes thought he missed his best friend just as much.

After three nights at the hotel with these frustrating, fleeting encounters, he was finally able to run her to ground early one morning. He had an early meeting at the fire station, and when he walked out of the side entrance near where he parked the vehicle he drove as fire chief—which was as much a mobile office as a mode of transportation—he spotted someone working in the scraggly flower beds that surrounded the inn.

The beds were mostly just a few tulips and some stubbly, rough-looking shrubs but it looked as if somebody was trying to make it more. Several flats of colorful blooms had been spaced with careful efficiency along the curvy sidewalk, ready to be transplanted into the flower beds.

At first, he assumed the gardener under the straw hat was someone from a landscaping service until he caught a glimpse of honey-blond hair.

He instantly switched direction. "Good morning," he called as he approached. She jumped and whirled around. When she spotted him, her instinctive look of surprise twisted into something that looked like dismay before she tucked it away and instead gave him a polite, impersonal smile.

"Oh. Hello."

If it didn't sting somewhere deep inside, he might have been amused at her cool tone.

"You do remember this is eastern Idaho, not Madrid, right? It's only April. We could have snow for another six weeks yet, easy."

"I remember," she answered stiffly. "These are all hardy early bloomers. They should be fine."

What he knew about gardening was, well, *nothing,* except how much he used to hate it when his mom would wake him and his brothers and Caidy up early to go out and weed her vegetable patch on summer mornings.

"If you say so. I would just hate to see you spend all this money on flowers and then wake up one morning to find a hard freeze has wiped them out overnight."

"I appreciate your concern for my wallet, but I've learned in thirty-one years on the earth that if you want to beautify the world around you a little bit, sometimes you have to take a few risks."

He could appreciate the wisdom in that, whether he was a gardener or not.

"I'm only working on the east- and south-facing beds for now, where there's less chance of frost kill. I might have been gone a few years, but I haven't quite forgotten the capricious weather we can see here in the Rockies."

What *had* she forgotten? She didn't seem to have too many warm memories of their time together, not if she could continue treating him with this annoyingly polite indifference.

He knew he needed to be heading to the station house for his meeting, but he couldn't resist lingering a moment with her to see if he could poke and prod more of a reaction out of her than this.

He looked around and had to point out the obvious. "No kids with you this morning?"

"They're inside fixing breakfast with my mother." She gestured to the small Craftsman-style cottage behind the inn where she had been raised. "I figured this was a good time to get something done before they come outside and my time will be spent trying to keep Alex from deciding he could dig a hole to China in the garden and Maya from picking every one of the pretty flowers."

He couldn't help smiling. Her kids were pretty darn cute—besides that, there was something so *right* about standing here with her while the morning sunlight glimmered in her hair and the cottonwood trees along the river sent out a few exploratory puffs on the sweet-smelling breeze.

"They're adorable kids."

She gave him a sidelong glance as if trying to gauge his sincerity. "When they're not starting fires, you mean?"

He laughed. "I'm going on the assumption that that was a fluke."

There. He saw it. The edges of her mouth quirked up and she almost smiled, but she turned her face away and he missed it.

He still considered it a huge victory. He always used to love making her smile.

Something stirred inside him as he watched her pick up a cheerful yellow flower and set it in the small hole she had just dug. Attraction, yes. Most definitely. He had forgotten how much he liked the way she looked, fresh and bright and as pretty as those flowers. Somehow he had also forgotten over the years that air of quiet grace and sweetness.

She was just as lovely as ever. No, that wasn't quite true. She was even more beautiful than she had been a decade ago. While he wasn't so sure how life in general had treated her, the years had been physically kind to her. With those big eyes and her high cheekbones and that silky hair he used to love burying his hands in, she was still beautiful. Actually, when he considered it, her beauty had more depth now than it did when she had been a young woman, and he found it even more appealing.

Yeah, he was every bit as attracted to her as he'd been in those days when thoughts of her had consumed him like the wildfires he used to fight every summer. But he'd been attracted to plenty of women in the past decade. What he felt right now, standing in the morning sunshine with Laura, ran much more deeply through him.

Unsettled and more than a little rattled by the sudden hot ache in his gut, he took the coward's way out and opted for the one topic he knew she wouldn't want to discuss. "What happened to the kids' father?"

She dumped a trowel full of dirt on the seedling with enough force to make him wince. "Remind me again why that's any of your business," she bit out.

"It's not. Only idle curiosity. You married him just a few years after you were going to marry me. You can't blame me for wondering about him."

She raised an eyebrow as if she didn't agree with that particular statement. "I'm sure you've heard the gory details," she answered, her voice terse. "Javier died six months ago. A boating accident off the coast of Barcelona. He and his mistress du jour were both killed. It was a great tragedy for everyone concerned."

Ah, hell. He knew her husband had died, but he hadn't heard the rest of it. He doubted anyone else in Pine Gulch had or the rumor would have certainly slithered its way toward him, given their history together.

She studiously refused to look at him. He knew her well enough to be certain she regretted saying anything and he couldn't help wondering why she had.

He also couldn't think of a proper response. How much pain did those simple words conceal?

"I'm sorry," he finally said, although it sounded lame and trite.

"About what? His death or the mistress?"

"Both."

Still avoiding his gaze, she picked up another flower start from the colorful flat. "He was a good father. Whatever else I could say about Javier, he loved his children. They both miss him very much."

"You don't?"

"Again, why is this your business?"

He sighed. "It's not. You're right. But we were best friends once, even before, well, everything, and I would still like to know about your life after you left here. I never stopped caring about you just because you dumped me."

Again, she refused to look at him. "Don't go there, Taft. We both know I only broke our engagement because you didn't have the guts to do it."

Oh. Ouch. Direct hit. He almost took a step back, but he managed to catch himself just in time. "Jeez, Laura, why don't you say what you really mean?" he managed to get out past the guilt and pain.

She rose to her feet, spots of color on her high cheekbones. "Oh, don't pretend you don't know what I'm talking about. You completely checked out of our relationship after your parents were murdered. Every time I tried to talk to you, you brushed me off, told me you were fine, then merrily headed to the Bandito for another drink and to flirt with some hot young thing there. I suppose it shouldn't have come as a surprise to anyone that I married a man who was unfaithful. You know what they say about old patterns being hard to break."

Well, she was talking to him. *Be careful what you wish for, Bowman.*

"I was *never* unfaithful to you."

She made a disbelieving sound. "Maybe you didn't actually go that far with another woman, but you sure seemed to enjoy being with all the Bandito bar babes much more than you did me."

This wasn't going at all the way he had planned when he stopped to talk to her. Moving into the inn and taking the temporary carpenter job had been one of his crazier ideas. Really, he had only wanted to test the waters and see if there was any chance of finding their way past the ugliness and anger to regain the friendship they had once shared, the friendship that had once meant everything to him.

Those waters were still pretty damn frigid.

She let out a long breath and looked as if she regretted bringing up the past. "I knew you wanted out, Taft. *Everyone* knew you wanted out. You just didn't want to hurt me. I understand and appreciate that."

"That's not how it happened."

"I was there. I remember it well. You were grieving and angry about your parents' murder. Anyone would be. It's completely understandable, which is why, if you'll remember, I wanted to postpone the wedding until you were in a better place. You wouldn't hear of it. Every time I brought it up, you literally walked away from me. How could I have married you under those circumstances? We both would have ended up hating each other."

"You're right. This way is much better, with only you hating me."

Un-freaking-believable. She actually looked hurt at that. "Who said I hated you?"

"*Hate* might be too big a word. *Despise* might be a little more appropriate."

She drew in a sharp breath. "I don't feel either of those things. The truth is, Taft, what we had together was a long time ago. I don't feel anything at all for you other than maybe a little fond nostalgia for what we once shared."

Oh. Double ouch. Pain sliced through him, raw and sharp. That was certainly clear enough. He was very much afraid it wouldn't take long for him to discover he was just as crazy about her as he had always been and all she felt in return was "fond nostalgia."

Or so she said anyway.

He couldn't help searching her expression for any hint that she wasn't being completely truthful, but she only gazed back at him with that same cool look, her mouth set in that frustratingly polite smile.

Damn, but he hated that smile. He suddenly wanted to lean forward, yank her against him and kiss away that smile until it never showed up there again.

Just for the sake of fond nostalgia.

Instead, he forced himself to give her a polite smile of his own and took a step in the direction of his truck.

He had a meeting and didn't want to be later than he already was.

"Good to know," he murmured. "I guess I had better let you get back to your gardening. My shift ends tonight at six and then I'm only on call for the next few days, so I should have a little more time to work on the rooms you're renovating. Leave me a list of jobs you would like me to do at the front desk. I'll try my best to stay out of your way."

There. That sounded cool and uninvolved.

If he slammed his truck door a little harder than strictly necessary, well, so what?

Chapter Four

When would she ever learn to keep her big mouth shut?

Long after Taft climbed into his pickup truck and drove away, Laura continued to yank weeds out of the sadly neglected garden beds with hands that shook while silently castigating herself for saying anything.

The moment she turned and found him walking toward her, she should have thrown down her trowel and headed back to the cottage.

Their conversation replayed over and over in her head. If her gardening gloves hadn't been covered in dirt, she would have groaned and buried her face in her hands.

First of all, why on earth had she told him about Javier and his infidelities? Taft was the *last* person in

Pine Gulch with whom she should have shared that particular tidbit of juicy information.

Even her mother didn't know how difficult the last few years of her marriage had become, how she would have left in an instant if not for the children and their adoration for Javier. Yet she had blurted the gory details right out to Taft, gushing her private heartache like a leaky sprinkler pipe.

So much for wanting him to think she had moved onward and upward after she left Pine Gulch. All she had accomplished was to make herself an object of pity in his eyes—as if she hadn't done that a decade ago by throwing all her love at someone who wasn't willing or capable at the time of catching it.

And then she had been stupid enough to dredge up the past, something she vowed she wouldn't do. Talking about it again had to have made him wonder if she were *thinking* about it, which basically sabotaged her whole plan to appear cool and uninterested in Taft.

He could always manage to get her to confide things she shouldn't. She had often thought he should have been the police officer, not his twin brother, Trace.

When she was younger, she used to tell him everything. They had talked about the pressure her parents placed on her to excel in school. About a few of the mean girls in her grade who had excluded her from their social circle because of those grades, about her first crush—on a boy other than him, of course. She didn't tell him that until much later.

They had probably known each other clear back in grade school, but she didn't remember much about him other than maybe seeing him around in the lunchroom, this big, kind of tough-looking kid who had an identical twin and who always smiled at everyone. He had been two whole grades ahead of her after all, in an entirely different social stratosphere.

Her first real memory of him was middle school, which in Pine Gulch encompassed seventh through ninth grades. She had been in seventh grade, Taft in ninth. He had been an athletic kid and well-liked, always able to make anyone laugh. She, on the other hand, had been quiet and shy, much happier with a book in her hand than standing by her locker with her friends between classes, giggling over the cute boys.

She and Taft had ended up both taking a Spanish elective and had been seated next to each other on Señora Baker's incomprehensible seating chart.

Typically, guys that age—especially jocks—didn't want to have much to do with younger girls. Gawky, insecure, bookish girls might as well just forget it. But somehow while struggling over past participles and conjugating verbs, they had become friends. She had loved his sense of humor and he seemed to appreciate how easily she picked up Spanish.

They had arranged study groups together for every test, often before school because Taft couldn't do it afterward most of the time due to practice sessions for whatever school sport he was currently playing.

She could remember exactly the first moment she knew she was in love with him. She had been in the library waiting for him early one morning. Because she lived in town and could easily walk to school, she was often there first. He and his twin brother usually caught a ride with their older brother, Ridge, who was a senior in high school at the time and had a very cool pickup truck with big tires and a roll bar.

While she waited for him, she had been fine-tuning a history paper due in a few weeks when Ronnie Lowery showed up. Ronnie was a jerk and a bully in her grade who had seemed to have it in for her for the past few years.

She didn't understand it but thought his dislike might have something to do with the fact that Ronnie's single mother worked as a housekeeper at the inn. Why that should bother Ronnie, she had no idea. His mom wasn't a very good maid and often missed work because of her drinking, but she had overheard her mom and dad talking once in the office. Her mom had wanted to fire Mrs. Lowery, but her dad wouldn't allow it.

"She's got a kid at home. She needs the job," her dad had said, which was exactly what she would have expected her dad to say. He had a soft spot for people down on their luck and often opened the inn to people he knew could never pay their tab.

She suspected Ronnie's mom must have complained about her job at home, which was likely the reason Ronnie didn't like her. He had tripped her a couple of times going up the stairs at school and once he had cornered her in the girls' bathroom and tried to kiss her and touch her chest—what little chest she had— until she had smacked him upside the head with her heavy advanced-algebra textbook and told him to keep his filthy hands off her, with melodramatic but firm effectiveness.

She usually did her best to avoid him whenever she

could, but that particular morning in seventh grade, she had been the only one in the school library. Even Mrs. Pitt, the plump and kind librarian who introduced her to Georgette Heyer books, seemed to have disappeared, she saw with great alarm.

Ronnie sat down. "Hey, Laura the whore-a."

"Shut up," she had said, very maturely, no doubt.

"Who's gonna make me?" he asked, looking around with exaggerated care. "I don't see anybody here at all."

"Leave me alone, Ronnie. I'm trying to study."

"Yeah, I don't think I will. Is that your history paper? You've got Mr. Olsen, right? Isn't that a coin-ki-dink? So do I. I bet we have the same assignment. I haven't started mine. Good thing, too, because now I don't have to."

He grabbed her paper, the one she had been working on every night for two weeks, and held it over his head.

"Give it back." She did her best not to cry.

"Forget it. You owe me for this. I had a bruise for two weeks after you hit me last month. I had to tell my mom I ran into the bleachers going after a foul ball in P.E."

"Want me to do it again?" she asked with much more bravado than true courage.

His beady gaze narrowed. "Try it, you little bitch, and I'll take more from you than just your freaking history paper."

"This history paper?"

At Taft's hard voice, all the tension coiled in her stomach like a rattlesnake immediately disappeared.

Ronnie was big for a seventh grader, but compared to Taft, big and tough and menacing, he looked like just what he was—a punk who enjoyed preying on people smaller than he was.

"Yes, it's mine," she blurted out. "I would like it back."

Taft had smiled at her, plucked the paper out of Ronnie's greasy fingers and handed it back to Laura.

"Thanks," she had mumbled.

"You're Lowery, right?" he said to Ronnie. "I think you've got P.E. with my twin brother, Trace."

"Yeah," the kid had muttered, though with a tinge of defiance in his voice.

"I'm sorry, Lowery, but you're going to have to move. We're studying for a Spanish test here. Laura is my tutor and I don't know what I would do if something happened to her. All I can say is, I would *not* be happy. I doubt my brother would be, either."

Faced with the possibility of the combined wrath of the formidable Bowman brothers, Ronnie had slunk away like the coward he was, and in that moment, Laura had known she would love Taft for the rest of her life.

He had moved on to high school the next year, of course, while she had been left behind in middle school to pine for him. Over the next two years, she remembered going to J.V. football games at the high school to watch him, sitting on the sidelines and keeping her fingers crossed that he would see her and smile.

Oh, yes. She had been plenty stupid when it came to Taft Bowman.

Finally, she had been in tenth grade and they would

once more be in the same school as he finished his senior year. She couldn't wait, that endless summer. To her eternal delight, when she showed up at her first hour, Spanish again, she had found Taft seated across the room.

She would never forget walking into the room and watching Taft's broad smile take over his face and how he had pulled his backpack off the chair next to him, as if he had been waiting just for her.

They hadn't dated that year. She had been too young and still in her awkward phase, and anyway, he had senior girls flocking around him all the time, but their friendship had picked up where it left off two years earlier.

He had confided his girl troubles to her and how he was trying to figure out whether to join the military like his brother planned to do, or go to college. Even though she had ached inside to tell him how she felt about him, she hadn't dared. Instead, she had listened and offered advice whenever he needed it.

He had ended up doing both, enrolling in college and joining the Army Reserve, and in the summers, he had left Pine Gulch to fight woodland fires. They maintained an email correspondence through it all and every time he came home, they would head to The Gulch to share a meal and catch up and it was as if they had never been apart.

And then everything changed.

Although a painfully late bloomer, she had finally developed breasts somewhere around the time she turned sixteen, and by the time she went to college, she had forced herself to reach outside her instinctive shyness. The summer after her freshman year of college when she had finally decided to go into hotel management, Taft had been fighting a fire in Oregon when he had been caught in a flare-up.

Everyone in town had been talking about it, how he had barely escaped with his life and had saved two other firefighters from certain death. The whole time, she had been consumed with worry for him.

Finally, he came back for a few weeks to catch up with his twin, who was back in Pine Gulch between military assignments, and she and Taft had gone for a late-evening horseback ride at the River Bow Ranch and he finally spilled out the story of the flare-up and how it was a miracle he was alive.

One minute he was talking to her about the fire, something she was quite certain he hadn't done with anyone else. The next—she still wasn't sure how it happened—he was kissing her like a starving man and she was a giant frosted cupcake.

They kissed for maybe ten minutes. She wasn't sure exactly how long, but she only knew they were the most glorious moments of her life. When he finally eased away from her, he had looked as horrified as if he had just accidentally stomped on a couple of kittens.

"I'm sorry, Laura. That was... Wow. I'm so sorry."

She remembered shaking her head, smiling at him, her heart aching with love. "What took you so blasted long, Taft Bowman?" she had murmured and reached out to kiss him again.

From that point on, they had been inseparable. She had been there to celebrate with him when he passed his EMT training, then paramedic training. He had visited her at school in Bozeman and made all her room-mates swoon. When she came home for summers, they would spend every possible moment together.

On her twenty-first birthday, he proposed to her. Even though they were both crazy-young, she couldn't have imagined a future without him and had finally agreed. She missed those times, that wild flutter in her stomach every time he kissed her.

She sighed now and realized with a little start of surprise that while she had been woolgathering, she had weeded all the way around to the front of the building that lined Main Street.

Her mom would probably be more than ready for her to come back and take care of the children. She stood and stretched, rubbing her cramped back, when she heard the rumble of a pickup truck pulling along-side her.

Oh, she hoped it wasn't Taft coming back. She was already off-balance enough from their encounter ear-lier and from remembering all those things she had purposely kept buried for years. When she turned, she saw a woman climbing out of the pickup and realized it was indeed a Bowman—his younger sister, Caidy.

"Hi, Laura! Remember me? Caidy Bowman."

"Of course I remember you," she exclaimed. Caidy rushed toward her, arms outstretched, and Laura just had time to shuck off her gardening gloves before she returned the other woman's embrace.

"How are you?" she asked.

Despite the six-year difference in their ages, they had been close friends and she had loved the idea of having Caidy for a sister when she married Taft.

Until their parents died, Caidy had been a fun, bright, openly loving teenager, secure in her position as the adored younger sister of the three older Bowman brothers. Everything changed after Caidy witnessed her parents' murder, Laura thought sadly.

"I'm good," Caidy finally answered. Laura hoped so. Those months after the murders had been rough on the girl. The trauma of witnessing the brutal deaths and being unable to do anything to stop them had left Caidy frightened to the point of helplessness. For several weeks, she refused to leave the ranch and had insisted on having one of her brothers present twenty-four hours a day.

Caidy and her grief had been another reason Laura had tried to convince Taft to postpone their June wedding, just six months after the murders, but he had insisted his parents wouldn't have wanted them to change their plans.

Not that any of that mattered now. Caidy had become a beautiful woman, with dark hair like her brothers' and the same Bowman green eyes.

"You look fantastic," Laura exclaimed.

Caidy made a face but hugged her again. "Same to you. Gosh, I can't believe it's been so long."

"What are you up to these days? Did you ever make it to vet school?"

Something flickered in the depths of her eyes but Caidy only shrugged. "No, I went to a couple semesters of school but decided college wasn't really for me. Since then, I've mostly just stuck around the ranch, helping Ridge with his daughter. I do a little training on the side. Horses and dogs."

"That's terrific," she said, although some part of her felt a little sad for missed opportunities. Caidy had always adored animals and had an almost uncanny rapport with them. All she used to talk about as a teenager was becoming a veterinarian someday and coming back to Pine Gulch to work.

One pivotal moment had changed so many lives, she thought. The violent murder of the Bowmans in a daring robbery of their extensive American West art collection had shaken everyone in town really. That sort of thing just didn't happen in Pine Gulch. The last murder the town had seen prior to that had been clear back in the 1930s when two ranch hands had fought it out over a girl.

Each of the Bowman siblings had reacted in different ways, she remembered. Ridge had thrown himself into the ranch and overseeing his younger siblings. Trace had grown even more serious and solemn. Caidy had withdrawn into herself, struggling with a completely natural fear of the world.

As for Taft, his answer had been to hide away his emotions and pretend everything was fine while inside he seethed with grief and anger and pushed away any of her attempts to comfort him.

"I'm looking for Taft," Caidy said now. "I had to make a run to the feed store this morning and thought I would stop and see if he wanted to head over to The Gulch for coffee and an omelet."

Oh, she loved The Gulch, the town's favorite diner. Why hadn't she been there since she returned to town? An image of the place formed clearly in her head—the tin-stamped ceiling, the round red swivel seats at the old-fashioned counter, the smell of frying bacon and coffee that had probably oozed into the paneling.

One of these mornings, she would have to take her children there.

"Taft isn't here. I'm sorry. He left about a half hour ago. I think he was heading to the fire station. He did say something about his shift ending at six."

"Oh. Okay. Thanks." Caidy paused a moment, tilting her head and giving Laura a long, inscrutable look very much like her brother would do. "I don't suppose you would like to go over to The Gulch with me and have breakfast, would you?"

She gazed at the other woman, as touched by the invitation as she was surprised. In all these years, Taft hadn't told his family that she had been the one to break their engagement? She knew he couldn't have. If Caidy knew, Laura had a feeling the other woman wouldn't be nearly as friendly.

The Bowmans tended to circle the wagons around their own.

That had been one of the hardest things about walking away from him. Her breakup with Taft had meant not only the loss of all her childish dreams but also the big, boisterous family she had always wanted as an only child of older parents who seemed absorbed with each other and their business.

For a moment, she was tempted to go to The Gulch with Caidy. Her mouth watered at the thought of Lou Archuleta's famous sweet rolls. Besides that, she would love the chance to catch up with Caidy. But before she could answer, her children came barreling out of the cottage, Maya in the lead for once but Alex close behind.

"Ma-ma! Gram made cakes. So good," Maya declared.

Alexandro caught up to his sister. "Pancakes, not cakes. You don't have cakes for breakfast, Maya. We're supposed to tell you to come in so you can wash up. Hurry! Grandma says I can flip the next one."

"Oh."

Caidy smiled at the children, clearly entranced by them.

"Caidy, this is my daughter, Maya, and my son, Alexandro. Children, this is my friend Caidy. She's Chief Bowman's sister."

"I like Chief Bowman," Alex declared. "He said if I start another fire, he's going to arrest me. Do you think he will?"

Caidy nodded solemnly. "Trust me, my brother never says anything he doesn't mean. You'll have to be certain not to start any more fires, then, won't you?"

"I know. I know. I already heard it about a million times. Hey, Mom, can I go so I can turn the pancakes with Grandma?"

She nodded and Alex raced back for the cottage with his sister in close pursuit.

"They're beautiful, Laura. Truly."

"I think so." She smiled and thought she saw a hint of something like envy in the other woman's eyes. Why didn't Caidy have a family of her own? she wondered. Was she still living in fear?

On impulse, she gestured toward the cottage. "Unless you have your heart set on cinnamon rolls down at The Gulch, why don't you stay and have breakfast here? I'm sure my mother wouldn't mind setting another plate for you."

Caidy blinked. "Oh, I couldn't."

"Why not? My mother's pancakes are truly delicious. In fact, a week from now, we're going to start offering breakfast at the inn to our guests. The plan is to start with some of Mom's specialties like pancakes and French toast but also to begin ordering some things from outside sources to showcase local businesses. I've already talked to the Java Hut about serving their coffee here and the Archuletas about offering some of The Gulch pastries to our guests."

"What a great idea."

"You can be our guinea pig. Come and have breakfast with us. I'm sure my mother will enjoy the company."

She would, too, she thought. She missed having a friend besides her mother. Her best friend in high school, besides Taft, had moved to Texas for her husband's job and Laura hadn't had a chance to connect with anyone else.

Even though she still emailed back and forth with her dearest friends and support system in Madrid, it wasn't the same as sharing coffee and pancakes and stories with someone who had known her for so long.

"I would love that," Caidy exclaimed. "Thank you. I'm sure Taft can find his own breakfast partner if he's so inclined."

From the rumors Laura had heard about the man in the years since their engagement, she didn't doubt that for a moment.

Chapter Five

To her relief, her children were charming and sweet with Caidy over breakfast. As soon as he found out their guest lived on a real-life cattle ranch, Alex peppered her with questions about cowboys and horses and whether she had ever seen a real-life Indian.

Apparently she had to have a talk with her son about political correctness and how reality compared to the American Westerns he used to watch avidly with their gnarled old housekeeper in Madrid.

Maya had apparently decided Caidy was someone she could trust, which was something of a unique occurrence. She sat beside her and gifted Taft's sister with her sweet smile and half of the orange Laura peeled for her.

"Thank you, sweetheart," Caidy said, looking touched by the gesture.

Whenever someone new interacted with Maya, Laura couldn't help a little clutch in her stomach, worry at how her daughter would be accepted.

She supposed that stemmed from Javier's initial reaction after her birth when the solemn-faced doctors told them Maya showed certain markers for Down syndrome and they were running genetic testing to be sure.

Her husband had been in denial for a long time and had pretended nothing was wrong. After all, how could he possibly have a child who wasn't perfect—by the world's standards anyway? Even after the testing revealed what Laura had already known in her heart, Javier has refused to discuss Maya's condition or possible outcomes.

Denial or not, he had still loved his daughter, though. She couldn't fault him for that. He was sometimes the only one who could calm the baby's crankiness and he had been infinitely calm with her.

Maya didn't quite understand that Javier was dead. She still had days when she asked over and over again where her papa was. During those rough patches, Laura would have to fight down deep-seated fury at her late husband.

Her children needed him and he had traded his future with them for the momentary pleasure he had found with his latest honey. Mingled with the anger and hurt was no small amount of guilt. If she had tried a little harder to open her heart to him and truly love him, maybe he wouldn't have needed to seek out other women.

She was doing her best, she reminded herself. Hadn't she traveled across the world to give them a home with family and stability?

"This was fun," Caidy said, drawing her back to the conversation. "Thank you so much for inviting me, but I probably better start heading back to the ranch. I've got a buyer coming today to look at one of the border collies I've been training."

"You're going to sell your dog?" Alex, who dearly wanted a puppy, looked horrified at the very idea.

"Sue isn't really my dog," Caidy explained with a smile. "I rescued her when she was a puppy and I've been training her to help someone else at their ranch. We have plenty of dogs at the River Bow."

Alex didn't seem to quite understand the concept of breeding and training dogs. "Doesn't it make you sad to give away your dog?"

Caidy blinked a little, but after a pause she nodded. "Yes, I guess it does a little. She's a good dog and I'll miss her. But I promise I'll make sure whoever buys her will give her a really good home."

"We have a good home, don't we, Grandma?" Alex appealed to Jan, who smiled.

"Why, yes, I believe we do, son."

"We can't have a dog right now, Alex."

Laura tried to head him off before he started extolling the virtues of their family like a used-car salesman trying to close a deal. "We've talked about this. While we're settling in here in Pine Gulch and living with Grandma here at the inn, it's just not practical."

He stuck out his lower lip, looking very much like his father when he couldn't get his way. "That's what you always say. I still really, really, really want a dog."

"Not now, Alexandro. We're not getting a dog. Maybe in a year or so when things here are a little more settled."

"But I want one now!"

"I'm sorry," Caidy said quickly, "but I'm afraid Sue wouldn't be very happy here. You see, she's a working dog and her very favorite thing is telling the cattle on our ranch which way we want them to go. You don't look very much like a steer. Where are your horns?"

Alex looked as if he wanted to ramp up to a full-fledged tantrum, something new since his father died, but he allowed himself to be teased out of it. "I'm not a steer," he said, rolling his eyes. Then a moment later he asked, "What's a steer?"

Caidy laughed. "It's another name for the male version of cow."

"I thought that was a bull."

"Uh." Caidy gave Laura a helpless sort of look.

While Jan snickered, Laura shook her head. "You're right. There are two kinds of male bovines, which is another word for cow. One's a bull and one is a steer."

"What's the difference?" he asked.

"Steers sing soprano," Caidy said. "And on that lovely note, I'd better get back to the bulls *and* steers of the River Bow. Thanks for a great breakfast. Next time it's my turn."

"Alex, will you and Maya help Gram with clearing the table while I walk Caidy out? I'll do the dishes when I come back inside."

To her relief, her son allowed himself to be distracted when Jan asked him if he and Maya would like to go to the park later in the day.

"I'm sorry about the near-tantrum there," she said as they headed outside to Caidy's pickup truck. "We're working on them, but my son still likes his own way."

"Most kids do. My niece is almost ten and she still thinks she should be crowned queen of the universe. I didn't mean to start something by talking about dogs."

"We've been having this argument for about three years now. His best friend in Madrid had this mangy old mutt, but Alex adored him and wanted one so badly. My husband would never allow it and for some reason Alex got it in his head after his father died that now there was no reason we couldn't get a dog."

"You're welcome to bring your kids out to the ranch sometime to enjoy my dogs vicariously. The kids might enjoy taking a ride, as well. We've got some pretty gentle ponies that would be perfect for them."

"That sounds fun. I'm sure they would both love it." She was quite certain this was one of those vague invitations that people said just to be polite, but to her surprise, Caidy didn't let the matter rest.

"How about next weekend?" she pressed. "I'm sure Ridge would be delighted to have you out."

Ridge was the Bowman sibling she had interacted with the least. At the time she was engaged to Taft, he and his parents weren't getting along, so he avoided the River Bow as much as possible. The few times she had met him, she had always thought him a little stern and humorless.

Still, he'd been nice enough to her—though the same couldn't have been said about his ex-wife, who had been rude and overbearing to just about everyone on the ranch.

"That's a lovely invitation, but I'm sure the last thing you need is to entertain a bunch of greenhorns."

"I would love it," Caidy assured her. "Your kids are just plain adorable and I can't tell you how thrilled I am that you're back in town. To tell you the truth, I'm a little desperate for some female conversation. At least something that doesn't revolve around cattle."

She should refuse. Her history with Taft had to make any interaction with the rest of the Bowmans more than a little awkward. But like Caidy, she welcomed any chance to resurrect their old friendship— and Alex and Maya *would* love the chance to ride horses and play with the ranch dogs.

"Yes, all right. The weekend would be lovely. Thank you."

"I'll call you Wednesday or Thursday to make some firm arrangements. This will be great!" Caidy beamed at her, looking fresh and pretty with her dark ponytail and sprinkling of freckles across the bridge of her nose.

The other woman climbed into her pickup truck and drove away with a wave and a smile and Laura watched after her for a moment, feeling much better about the morning than she had when the previous Bowman sibling had driven away from the inn.

* * *

Taft had visitors.

The whir of the belt sander didn't quite mask the giggles and little scurrying sounds from the doorway. He made a show of focusing on the window he was framing while still maintaining a careful eye on the little creatures who would occasionally peek around the corner of the doorway and then hide out of sight again.

He didn't want to let his guard down, not with all the power equipment in here. He could just imagine Laura's diatribe if one of her kids somehow got hurt. She would probably accuse him of letting her rambunctious older kid cut off his finger on purpose.

The game of peekaboo lasted for a few more minutes until he shut off the belt sander. He ran a finger over the wood to be sure the frame was smooth before he headed over to the window to hold it up for size, keeping an eye on the door the whole time.

"Go on," he heard a whispered voice say, then giggles, and a moment later he was joined by Laura's daughter.

Maya. She was adorable, with that dusky skin, curly dark hair in pigtails and Laura's huge blue eyes, almond-shaped on Maya.

"Hola," she whispered with a shy smile.

"Hola, señorita," he answered. Apparently he still remembered a *little* of the high-school Spanish he had struggled so hard to master.

"What doing?" she asked.

"I'm going to put some new wood up around this

window. See?" He held the board into the intended place to demonstrate, then returned it to the worktable.

"Why?" she asked, scratching her ear.

He glanced at the doorway where the boy peeked around, then hid again like a shadow.

"The old wood was rotting away. This way it will look much nicer. More like the rest of the room."

That face peeked around the doorway again and this time Taft caught him with an encouraging smile. After a pause, the boy sidled into the room.

"Loud," Maya said, pointing to the belt sander with fascination.

"It can be. I've got things to block your ears if you want them."

He wasn't sure she would understand, but she nodded vigorously, so he reached for his ear protectors on top of his toolbox. The adult-size red ear guards were huge on her—the bottom of the cups hit her at about shoulder height. He reached out to work the slide adjustment on top. They were still too big but at least they covered most of her ears.

She beamed at him, pleased as punch, and he had to chuckle. "Nice. You look great."

"I see," she said, and headed unerringly for the mirror hanging on the back of the bathroom door, where she turned her head this way and that, admiring her headgear as if he had given her a diamond tiara.

Oh, she was a heartbreaker, this one.

"Can I use some?" Alexandro asked, from about two feet away, apparently coaxed all the way into the room by what his sister was wearing.

"I'm afraid I've got only the one pair. I wasn't expecting company. Sorry. Next time I'll remember to pack a spare. I probably have regular earplugs in my toolbox."

Alex shrugged. "That's okay. I don't mind the noise. Maya freaks at loud noises, but I don't care."

"Why is that? Maya, I mean, and loud noises?"

The girl was wandering around the room, humming to herself loudly, apparently trying to hear herself through the ear protection.

The kid looked fairly protective himself, watching over his sister as she moved from window to window. "She just does. Mom says it's because she has so much going on inside her head she sometimes forgets the rest of us and loud noises startle her into remembering. Or something like that."

"You love your sister a lot, don't you?"

"She's my sister." He shrugged, looking suddenly much older than his six years. "I have to watch out for her and Mama now that our papa is gone."

Taft wanted to hug him, too, and he had to fight down a lump in his throat. He thought about his struggle when his parents had died. He had been twenty-four years old. Alex was just a kid and had already lost his father, but he seemed to be handling it with stoic grace. "I bet you do a great job, protecting them both."

The boy looked guilty. "Sometimes. I didn't on the day of the fire."

"We've decided that was an accident, right? It's over and you're not going to do it again. Take it from me, kid. Don't beat yourself up over past mistakes. Just move on and try to do better next time."

Alex didn't look as if he quite understood. Why

should he? Taft rolled his eyes at himself. Philosophy and six-year-old boys didn't mix all that well.

"Want to try your hand with the sander?" he asked.

Alex's blue eyes lit up. "Really? Is it okay?"

"Sure. Why not? Every guy needs to know how to run a belt sander."

Before beginning the lesson, Taft thought it wise to move toward Maya, who was sitting on the floor some distance away, drawing her finger through the sawdust mess he hadn't had time to clear up yet. Her mom would probably love that, but because she was already covered, he decided he would clean her up when they were done.

He lifted one of the ear protectors away from her ear so he could talk to her. "Maya, we're going to turn on the sander, okay?"

"Loud."

"It won't be when you have this on. I promise."

She narrowed her gaze as if she were trying to figure out whether to believe him, then she nodded and returned to the sawdust. He gazed at the back of her head, tiny compared to the big ear guards, and was completely bowled over by her ready trust.

Now he had to live up to it.

He turned on the sander, hoping the too-big ear protectors would still do their job. Maya looked up, a look of complete astonishment on her cute little face. She pulled one ear cup away, testing to see if the sander was on, but quickly returned it to the original position. After a minute, she pulled it away again and then replaced it, a look of wonder on her face at the magic of safety wear.

He chuckled and turned back to Alex, waiting eagerly by the belt sander.

"Okay, the most important thing here is that we don't sand your fingers off. I'm not sure your mom would appreciate that."

"She wouldn't," Alex assured him with a solemn expression.

Taft had to fight his grin. "We'll have to be careful, then. Okay. Now you always start up the belt sander before you touch it to the wood so you don't leave gouges. Right here is the switch. Now keep your hands on top of mine and we can do it together. That's it."

For the next few minutes, they worked the piece of wood until he was happy with the way it looked and felt. He always preferred to finish sanding his jobs the old-fashioned way, by hand, but a belt sander was a handy tool for covering a large surface quickly and efficiently.

When they finished, he carefully turned off the belt sander and set it aside, then returned to the board and the boy. "Okay, now here's the second most important part, after not cutting your fingers off. We have to blow off the sawdust. Like this."

He demonstrated with a puff of air, then handed the board to the boy, who puckered up and blew as if he were the big, bad wolf after the three little pigs.

"Perfect," Taft said with a grin. "Feel how smooth that is now?"

The boy ran his finger along the wood grain. "Wow! I did that?"

"Absolutely. Good job. Now every time you come

into this room, you can look out through the window and remember you helped frame it up."

"Cool! Why do you have to sand the wood?"

"When the wood is smooth, it looks better and you get better results with whatever paint or varnish you want to use on it."

"How does the sander thingy work?"

"The belt is made of sandpaper. See? Because it's rough, when you rub it on the wood, it works away the uneven surface."

"Can you sand other things besides wood?" he asked.

Taft had to laugh at the third degree. "You probably can but it's made for wood. It would ruin other things. Most tools have a specific purpose and when you use them for something else, you can cause more problems."

"Me," an abnormally loud voice interrupted before Alex could ask any more questions. With the ear protectors, Maya obviously couldn't judge the decibel level of her own voice. "I go now."

"Okay, okay. You don't need to yell about it," Alex said, rolling his eyes in a conspiratorial way toward Taft.

Just like that, both of these kids slid their way under his skin, straight to his heart, partly because they were Laura's, but mostly because they were just plain adorable.

"Can I?" she asked, still speaking loudly.

He lifted one of the ear protectors so she could hear him. "Sure thing, sweetheart. I've got another board that needs sanding. Come on."

Alex looked disgruntled, but he backed away to give his sister room. Taft was even more careful with Maya, keeping his hands firmly wrapped around hers on the belt sander as they worked the wood.

When they finished, he removed her earwear completely. "Okay, now, like I told your brother, this is the most important part. I need you to blow off the sawdust."

She puckered comically and puffed for all she was worth and he helped her along. "There. Now feel what we did."

"Ooh. Soft." She smiled broadly at him and he returned her smile, just as he heard their names.

"Alex? Maya? Where are you?"

Laura's voice rang out from down the hall, sounding harried and a little hoarse, as if she had been calling for a while.

The two children exchanged looks, as if they were bracing themselves for trouble.

"That's our mama," Alex said unnecessarily.

"Yeah, I heard."

"Alex? Maya? Come out this instant."

"They're in here," he called out, although some part of him really didn't want to take on more trouble. He thought of their encounter a few days earlier when she had looked so fresh and pretty while she worked on the inn's flower gardens—and had cut into his heart more effectively than if she had used her trowel.

She charged into the room, every inch the concerned mother. "What's going on? Why didn't you two answer me? I've been calling through the whole hotel."

Taft decided to take one for the team. "I'm afraid

that's my fault. We had the sander going. We couldn't hear much up here."

"Look, Mama. Soft." Maya held up the piece of wood she had helped him sand. "Feel!"

Laura stepped closer, reluctance in her gaze. He was immediately assailed by the scent of her, of flowers and springtime.

She ran a hand along the wood, much as her daughter had. "Wow. That's great."

"I did it," Maya declared.

Laura arched an eyebrow. She managed to look huffy and disapproving at him for just a moment before turning back to her daughter with what she quickly transformed into an interested expression. "Did you, now? With the power sander and everything?"

"I figured I would let them run the circular saw next," he said. "Really, what's the worst that can happen?"

She narrowed her gaze at him as if trying to figure out if he was teasing. Whatever happened to her sense of humor? he wondered. Had he robbed her of that or had it been her philandering jackass of a husband?

"I'm kidding," he said. "I was helping them the whole way. Maya even wore ear protection, didn't you? Show your mom."

The girl put on her headgear and started singing some made-up song loudly, pulling the ear guards away at random intervals.

"Oh, that looks like great fun," Laura said, taking the ear protectors off her daughter and handing them to Taft. Their hands brushed as he took them from her and a little charge of electricity arced between them, sizzling right to his gut.

She pulled her hands away quickly and didn't meet his gaze. "You shouldn't be up here bothering Chief Bowman. I told you to stay away when he's working."

And why would she think she had to do that? he wondered, annoyed. Did she think he couldn't be trusted with her kids? He was the Pine Gulch fire chief, for heaven's sake, and a trained paramedic to boot. Public safety was sort of his thing.

"It was fun," Alex declared. "I got to use the sander first. Feel my board now, Mama."

She appeared to have no choice but to comply. "Nice job. But next time you need to listen to me and not bother Chief Bowman while he's working."

"I didn't mind," Taft said. "They're fun company."

"You're busy. I wouldn't want them to be a bother."

"What if they're not?"

She didn't look convinced. "Come on, you two. Tell Chief Bowman thank-you for letting you try out the dangerous power tools, after you promise him you'll never touch any of them on your own."

"We promise," Alex said dutifully.

"Promise," his sister echoed.

"Thanks for showing me how to use a sander," Alex said. "I need one of those."

Now *there* was a disaster in the making. But because the kid wasn't his responsibility, as his mother had made quite clear, he would let Laura deal with it.

"Thanks for helping me," he said. "I couldn't have finished without you two lending a hand."

"Can I help you again sometime?" the boy asked eagerly.

Laura tensed beside him and he knew she wanted him to say no. It annoyed the heck out of him and he wanted to agree, just to be contrary, but he couldn't bring himself to blatantly go against her wishes.

Instead, he offered the standard adult cop-out even though it grated. "We'll have to see, kiddo," he answered.

"Okay, now that you've had a chance with the power tools, take your sister and go straight down to the front desk to your grandmother. No detours, Alex. Got it?"

His stubborn little chin jutted out. "But we were having fun."

"Chief Bowman is trying to get some work done. He's not here to babysit."

"I'm not a baby," Alex grumbled.

Laura bit back what Taft was almost certain was a smile. "I know you're not. It's just a word, *mi hijo*. Either way, you need to take your sister straight down to the lobby to find your grandmother."

With extreme reluctance in every step, Alex took his little sister's hand and led her out the door and down the hall, leaving Laura alone with him.

Even though he could tell she wasn't thrilled to have found her children there with him and some part of him braced himself to deal with her displeasure, another, louder part of him was just so damn happy to see her again.

Ridiculous, he knew, but he couldn't seem to help it. How had he forgotten that little spark of happiness that always seemed to jump in his chest when he saw her after an absence of just about any duration?

Even with her hair in a ponytail and an oversize shirt and faded jeans, she was beautiful, and he wanted to stand here amid the sawdust and clutter and just savor the sight of her.

As he might have expected, she didn't give him much of a chance. "Sorry about the children," she said stiffly. "I thought they were watching *SpongeBob* in the bedroom of Room Twelve while I cleaned the bathroom grout. I came out of the bathroom and they were gone, which is, unfortunately, not all that uncommon with my particular kids."

"Next time maybe you should use the security chain to keep them contained," he suggested, only half-serious.

Even as he spoke, he was aware of a completely inappropriate urge to wrap her in his arms and absorb all her cares and worries about wandering children and tile grout and anything else weighing on her.

"A great idea, but unfortunately I've already tried that. Within about a half hour, Alex figured out how to lift his sister up and have her work the chain free. They figured out the dead bolt in about half that time. I just have to remember I can't take my eyes off them for a second. I'll try to do a better job of keeping them out of your way."

"I told you, I don't mind them. Why would I? They're great kids." He meant the words, even though his previous experience with kids, other than the annual fire-safety lecture he gave at the elementary school, was mostly his niece, Destry, Ridge's daughter.

"I think they're pretty great," she answered.

"That Alex is a curious little guy with a million questions."

She gave a rueful sigh and tucked a strand of hair behind her delicate ear. She used to love it when he kissed her neck, just there, he remembered, then wished the memory had stayed hidden as heat suddenly surged through him.

"Yes, I'm quite familiar with my son's interrogation technique," Laura said, oblivious to his reaction, thank heavens. "He's had six years to hone them well."

"I don't mind the questions. Trace and I were both the same way when we were kids. My mom used to say that between the two of us, we didn't give her a second to even catch a breath between questions."

She trailed her fingers along the wood trim and he remembered how she used to trail them across his stomach....

"I remember some of the stories your mother used to tell me about you and Trace and the trouble you could get into. To be honest with you, I have great sympathy with your mother. I can't imagine having two of Alex."

He dragged his mind away from these unfortunate memories that suddenly crowded out rational thought. "He's a good boy, just has a lot of energy. And that Maya. She's a heartbreaker."

She pulled her hand away from the wood, her expression suddenly cold. "Don't you dare pity her."

"Why on earth would I do that?" he asked, genuinely shocked.

She frowned. "Because of her Down syndrome. Many people do."

"Then you shouldn't waste your time with them. Down syndrome or not, she's about the sweetest thing I've ever seen. You should have seen her work the belt sander, all serious and determined, chewing on her lip in concentration—just like you used to do when you were studying."

"Don't."

He blinked, startled at her low, vehement tone. "Don't what?"

"Try to charm me by acting all sweet and concerned. It might work on your average bimbo down at the Bandito, but I'm not that stupid."

Where did *that* come from? "Are you kidding? You're about the smartest person I know. I never thought you were stupid."

"That makes one of us," she muttered, then looked as if she regretted the words.

More than anything, he wanted to go back in time ten years and make things right again with her. He had hurt her by closing her out of his pain, trying to deal with the grief and guilt in his own way.

But then, she had hurt him, too. If only she had given him a little more time and trusted that he would work things through, he would have figured everything out eventually. Instead, she had gone away to Spain and met her jerk of a husband—and had two of the cutest kids he had ever met.

"Laura—" he began, not sure what he intended to say, but she shook her head briskly.

"I'm sorry my children bothered you. I won't let it happen again."

"I told you, I don't mind them."

"I mind. I don't want them getting attached to you when you'll be in their lives for only a brief moment."

He hadn't even known her kids a week ago. So why did the idea of not seeing them again make his chest ache? Uneasy with the reaction, he gave her a long look.

"For someone who claims not to hate me, you do a pretty good impression of it. You don't even want me around your kids, like I'll contaminate them somehow."

"You're exaggerating. You're virtually a stranger to me after all this time. I don't hate you. I feel nothing at all for you. Less than nothing."

He moved closer to her, inhaling the springtime scent of her shampoo. "Liar."

The single word was a low hush in the room and he saw her shiver as if he had trailed his finger down her cheek.

She started to take a step back, then checked the motion. "Oh, get over yourself," she snapped. "Yes, you broke my heart. I was young and foolish enough to think you meant what you said, that you loved me and wanted forever with me. We were supposed to take vows about being with each other in good times and bad, but you wouldn't share the bad with me. Instead, you started drinking and hanging out at the Bandito and pretending nothing was wrong. I was devastated. I won't make a secret of that. I thought I wouldn't survive the pain."

"I'm sorry," he said.

She made a dismissive gesture. "I should really thank you, Taft. If not for that heartbreak, I would have been only a weak, silly girl who would probably have become a weak, silly woman. Instead, I became stronger. I took my broken heart and turned it into a grand adventure in Europe, where I matured and experienced the world a little bit instead of just Pine Gulch, and now I have two beautiful children to show for it."

"Why did you give up on us so easily?"

Her mouth tightened with anger. "You know, you're right. I should have gone ahead with the wedding and then just waited around wringing my hands until you decided to pull your head out of whatever crevice you jammed it into. Although from the sound of it, I might still have been waiting, ten years later."

"I'm sorry for hurting you," he said, wishing again that he could go back and change everything. "More sorry than I can ever say."

"Ten years too late," she said tersely. "I told you, it doesn't matter."

"It obviously does or you wouldn't bristle like a porcupine every time you're near me."

"I don't—" she started to say, but he cut her off.

"I don't blame you. I was an ass to you. I'll be the first to admit it."

"The second," she said tartly.

If this conversation didn't seem so very pivotal, he might have smiled, but he had the feeling he had the chance to turn things around between them right here and now, and he wanted that with a fierce and powerful need.

"Probably. For what it's worth, my family would fill out the rest of the top five there, waiting in line to call me names."

She almost smiled but she hid it quickly. What would it take for him to squeeze a real smile out of her and keep it there? he wondered.

"I know we can't go back and change things," he said slowly. "But what are the chances that we can at least be civil to each other? We were good friends once, before we became more. I miss that."

She was quiet for several moments and he was aware of the random sounds of the old inn. The shifting of old wood, the creak of a floorboard somewhere, a tree branch that needed to be pruned back rattling against the thin glass of the window.

When she spoke, her voice was low. "I miss it, too," she said, in the tone of someone confessing a rather shameful secret.

Something inside him seemed to uncoil at her words. He gazed at her so-familiar features that he had once known as well as his own.

The high cheekbones, the cute little nose, those blue eyes that always reminded him of his favorite columbines that grew above the ranch. He wanted to kiss her, with a raw ferocity that shocked him to his toes. To sink into her and not climb out again.

He managed, just barely, to restrain himself and was grateful for it when she spoke again, her voice just above a whisper.

"We can't go back, Taft."

"No, but we can go forward. That's better anyway, isn't it? The reality is, we're both living in the same small town. Right now we're living at the same address, for Pete's sake. We can't avoid each other. But that doesn't mean we need to go on with this awkwardness between us, does it? I would really like to see if together we can find some way to move past it. What do you say?"

She gazed at him for a long moment, uncertainty in those eyes he loved so much. Finally she seemed to come to some internal decision.

"Sure. We can try to be friends again." She gave him a tentative smile. A real one this time, not that polite thing he had come to hate, and his chest felt tight and achy all over again.

"I need to get back to work. I'll see you later."

"Goodbye, Laura," he said.

She gave him one more little smile before hurrying out of the room. He watched her go, more off-balance by the encounter with Laura and her children than he wanted to admit. As he turned back to his work, he was also aware of a vague sense of melancholy that made no sense. This was progress, right? Friendship was a good place to start—hadn't their relationship begun out of friendship from the beginning?

He picked up another board from the pile. He knew the source of his discontent. He wanted more than friendship with Laura. He wanted what they used to have, laughter and joy and that contentment that seemed to seep through him every time he was with her.

Baby steps, he told himself. He could start with friendship and then gradually build on that, see how things progressed. Nothing wrong with a little patience once in a while.

Her hands were still shaking as Laura walked out of the room and down the hall. She headed for the lobby, with the curving old stairs and the classic light fixtures that had probably been installed when Pine Gulch finally hit the electrical grid.

Only when she was certain she was completely out of sight of Taft did she lean against the delicately flowered wallpaper and press a hand to her stomach.

What an idiot she was, as weak as a baby lamb around him. She always had been. Even if she had hours of other more urgent homework, if Taft called her and needed help with Spanish, she would drop everything to rush to his aid.

It didn't help matters that the man was positively dangerous when he decided to throw out the charm.

Oh, it would be so easy to give in, to let all that seductive charm slide around and through her until she forgot all the reasons she needed to resist him.

He asked if they could find a way to friendship again. She didn't have the first idea how to answer that. She wanted to believe her heart had scarred over from the disappointment and heartache, the loss of those dreams for the future, but she was more than a little afraid to peek past the scars to see if it had truly healed.

She was tough and resilient. Hadn't she survived a bad marriage and then losing the husband she had tried to love? She could surely carry on a civil conversation with Taft on the rare occasions they met in Pine Gulch.

What was the harm in it? For heaven's sake, re-establishing a friendly relationship with the man didn't mean she was automatically destined to tumble head-long back into love with him.

Life in Pine Gulch would be much easier all the way around if she didn't feel jumpy and off-balance every time she was around him.

She eased away from the wallpaper and straight-ened her shirt that had bunched up. This was all ri-diculous anyway. What did it matter if she was weak around him? She likely wouldn't ever have the oppor-tunity to test out her willpower. From the rumors she heard, Taft probably had enough young, hot bar babes at the Bandito that he probably couldn't be bothered with a thirty-two-year-old widow with two children, one of whom with a disability that would require life-long care.

She wasn't the same woman she had been ten years ago. She had given birth to two kids and had the body to show for it. Her hair was always messy and falling out of whatever clip she had shoved it in that morning, half the time she didn't have time to put on makeup until she had been up for hours and, between the kids and the inn, she was perpetually stressed.

Why on earth would a man like Taft, gorgeous and masculine, want anything *but* friendship with her these days?

She wasn't quite sure why that thought depressed her and made her feel like that gawky seventh grader with braces crushing on a ninth-grade athlete who was nice to her.

Surely she didn't *want* to have to resist Taft Bowman. It was better all around if he saw her merely as that frumpy mother.

She knew that was probably true, even as some ecret, silly little part of her wanted to at least have the *chance* to test her willpower around him.

Chapter Six

"Hurry, Mama." Alex practically jumped out of his booster seat the moment she turned off the engine at the River Bow Ranch on Saturday. "I want to see the dogs!"

"Dogs!" Maya squealed after him, wiggling and tugging against the car-seat straps. The only reason she didn't rush to join her brother outside the car was her inability to undo the straps on her own, much to her constant frustration.

"Hang on, you two." Their excitement made her smile, despite the host of emotions churning through her at visiting the River Bow again for the first time in a decade. "The way you're acting, somebody might think you'd never seen a dog before."

"I have, too, seen a dog before," Alex said. "But this

isn't just *one* dog. Miss Bowman said she had a *lot* of dogs. And horses, too. Can I really ride one?"

"That's the plan for now, but we'll have to see how things go." She was loath to make promises about things that were out of her control. Probably a fallback to her marriage, those frequent times when the children would be so disappointed if their father missed dinner or a school performance or some special outing.

"I hope I *can* ride a horse. Oh, I hope so." Alex practically danced around the used SUV she had purchased with the last of her savings when she arrived back in the States. She had to smile at his enthusiasm as she unstrapped Maya and lifted her out of the vehicle.

Maya threw her chubby little arms around Laura's neck before she could set her on the ground.

"Love you," her daughter said.

The spontaneously affectionate gesture turned her insides to warm mush, something her sweet Maya so often did. "Oh, I love you, too, darling. More than the moon and the stars and the sea."

"Me, too," Alex said.

She hugged him with the arm not holding Maya. "I love you both. Aren't I the luckiest mom in the world to have two wonderful kiddos to love?"

"Yes, you are," he said, with a total lack of vanity that made her smile.

She supposed she couldn't be a completely terrible mother if she was raising her children with such solid assurance of their place in her heart.

At the sound of scrabbling paws and panting

breaths, she raised her head from her children. "Guess what? Here come the dogs."

Alex whirled around in time to see Caidy approaching them with three dogs shadowing her. Laura identified two of them as border collies, mostly black with white patches on their faces and necks, quizzical ears and eerily intelligent expressions. The third was either a breed she didn't recognize or some kind of mutt of undetermined origin, with reddish fur and a German shepherd–like face.

Maya stiffened nervously, not at all experienced around dogs, and tightened her arms around Laura's neck. Alex, on the other hand, started to rush toward the dogs, but Laura checked him with a hand on his shoulder.

"Wait until Caidy says it's safe," she ordered her son, who would run directly into a lion's enclosure if he thought he might have a chance of petting the creature.

"Perfectly safe," Caidy assured them.

Taft's sister wore jeans and a bright yellow T-shirt along with boots and a straw cowboy hat, her dark hair braided down her back. She looked fresh and pretty as she gave them all a welcoming smile. "The only danger from my dogs is being licked to death—or maybe getting knocked over by a wagging tail."

Alex giggled and Caidy looked delighted at the sound.

"Your mother is right, though," she said. "You should never approach any strange animal without permission until you know it's safe."

"Can I pet one?"

"Sure thing. King. Forward."

One of the lean black-and-white border collies obeyed and sidled toward them, sniffing eagerly at Alex's legs. The boy giggled and began to pet the dog with sheer joy.

"This was such a great idea," Laura said, smiling as she watched her son. "Thank you so much for the invitation, Caidy."

"You're welcome. Believe me, it will be a fun break for me from normal ranch stuff. Spring is always crazy on the ranch and I've been looking forward to this all week as a great respite."

She paused. "I have to tell you, I'm really glad you're still willing to have anything to do with the Bowmans after the way things ended with Taft."

She really didn't want to talk about Taft. This was what she had worried about after Caidy extended the invitation, that things might be awkward between them because of the past.

"Why wouldn't I? Taft and I are still friendly." And that's all they ever *would* be, she reminded herself. "Just because he and I didn't end up the way we thought we would doesn't mean I should shun his family. I loved your family. I'm only sorry I haven't stayed in touch all these years. I see no reason we can't be friends now, unless you're too uncomfortable because of…everything?"

"Not at all!" Caidy exclaimed. Laura had the impression she wanted to say something else, but Alex interrupted before she could.

"He licked me. It tickles!"

Caidy grinned down at the boy's obvious enjoyment of the dogs. He now had all three dogs clustered around him and was petting them in turns.

"We've got puppies. Would you like to see them?" Caidy asked.

"Puppies!" Maya squealed, still in her arms, while Alex clasped his hands together, a reverential look on his face.

"Puppies! Oh, Mama, can we?"

She had to laugh at his flair for drama. "Sure. Why not? As long as it's all right with Caidy."

"They're in the barn. I was just checking on the little family a few minutes ago and it looks like a few of the pups are awake and might just be in the mood to play."

"Oh, yay!" Alex exclaimed and Caidy grinned at him.

They followed her into the barn. For Laura, it was like walking back in time. The barn smelled of hay and leather and animals, and the familiar scent mix seemed to trigger an avalanche of memories. They tumbled free of whatever place she'd stowed them after she walked away from Pine Gulch, jostling and shoving their way through her mind before she had a chance to block them out.

She used to come out to the ranch often to ride horses with Taft and their rides always started here, in the barn, where he would teach her about the different kinds of tack and how each was used, then patiently give her lessons on how to tack up a horse.

One wintry January afternoon, she suddenly re-membered, she had helped him and his father deliver a foal. She could still vividly picture her astonishment at the gangly, awkward miracle of the creature.

Unbidden, she also remembered that the relative privacy of the barn compared to other places on the ranch had been one of their favorite places to kiss. Sultry, long, intense kisses that would leave them both hungry for more....

She absolutely did not need to remember *those* particular memories, full of heat and discovery and that all-consuming love that used to burn inside her for Taft. With great effort, she struggled to wrestle them back into the corner of her mind and slam the door to them so she could focus on her children and Caidy and new puppies.

The puppies' home was an empty stall at the end of the row. An old russet saddle blanket took up one corner and the mother dog, a lovely black-and-white heeler, was lying on her side taking a rest and watching her puppies wrestle around the straw-covered floor of the stall. She looked up when Caidy approached and her tail slapped a greeting.

"Hey, Betsy, here I am again. How's my best girl? I brought some company to entertain your pups for a while."

Laura could swear she saw understanding and even relief in the dog's brown eyes as Caidy unlatched the door of the stall and swung it out. She could relate to that look—every night when her children finally closed their eyes, she would collapse onto the sofa with probably that same sort of look.

"Are you sure it's okay?" Alex asked, standing outside the stall, barely containing his nervous energy.

"Perfectly sure," Caidy answered. "I promise, they love company."

He headed inside and—just as she might have predicted—Maya wriggled to get down. "Me, too," she insisted.

"Of course, darling," Laura said. She set her on her feet and the girl headed inside the stall to stand beside her brother.

"Here, sit down and I'll bring you a puppy each," Caidy said, gesturing to a low bench inside the stall, really just a plank stretched across a couple of overturned oats buckets.

She picked up a fat, waddling black-and-white puppy from the writhing, yipping mass and set it on Alex's lap, then reached into the pile again for a smaller one, mostly black this time.

Now she had some very different but infinitely precious memories of this barn to add to her collection, Laura thought a few moments later. The children were enthralled with the puppies. Children and puppies just seemed to go together like peanut butter and jelly. Alex and Maya giggled as the puppies squirmed around on their laps, licking and sniffing. Maya hugged hers as enthusiastically as she had hugged her mother a few minutes earlier.

"Thank you for this," she said to Caidy as the two of them smiled at the children and puppies. "You've thrilled them to their socks."

"I'm afraid the pups are a little dirty and don't smell the greatest. They're a little young for baths yet."

"I don't worry about a little dirt," Laura said. "I've

always figured if my kids don't get dirty sometimes, I'm doing something wrong."

"I don't think you're doing *anything* wrong," Caidy assured her. "They seem like great kids."

"Thank you."

"It can't be easy, especially now that you're on your own."

As much as Javier had loved the children, she had always felt very much on her own in Madrid. He was always busy with the hotel and his friends and, of course, his other women. Bad enough she had shared that with Taft. She certainly wasn't about to share that information with his sister.

"I have my mother to help me now. She's been a lifesaver."

Coming home had been the right decision. As much as she had struggled with taking her children away from half of their heritage probably forever, Javier's family had never been very welcoming to her. They had become even less so after Maya was born, as if Laura were to blame somehow for the genetic abnormality.

"I'm just going to come out and say this, okay?" Caidy said after a moment. "I really wish you had married Taft so we could have been sisters."

"Thank you," she said, touched by the words.

"I mean it. You were the best thing that ever happened to him. We all thought so. Compared to the women he… Well, compared to anybody else he's dated, you're a million times better. I still can't believe any brother of mine was stupid enough to let you slip through his fingers. Don't think I haven't told him so, too."

She didn't know quite how to answer—or why she had this sudden urge to protect him. Taft hadn't been stupid, only hurt and lost and not at all ready for marriage.

She hadn't been ready, either, although it had taken her a few years to admit that to herself. At twenty-one, she had been foolish enough to think her love should have been enough to help him heal from the pain and anger of losing his parents in such a violent way, when he hadn't even had the resolution of the murderers being caught and brought to justice.

An idealistic, romantic young woman and an angry, bitter young man would have made a terrible combination, she thought as she sat here in this quiet barn while the puppies wriggled around with her children and a horse stamped and snorted somewhere nearby.

"I also have a confession." Caidy shifted beside her at the stall door.

She raised an eyebrow. "Do I really want to hear this?"

"Please don't be mad, okay?"

For some reason, Laura was strongly reminded of Caidy as she had known her a decade ago, the light-hearted, mischievous teenager who thought she could tease and cajole her way out of any situation.

"Tell me. What did you do?" she asked, amusement fighting the sudden apprehension curling through her.

Before the other woman could answer, a male voice rang out through the barn. "Caidy? Are you in here?"

Her stomach dropped and the little flutters of apprehension became wild-winged flaps of anxiety.

Caidy winced. "Um, I may have casually mentioned to Taft that you and the children were coming out to the ranch today and that we might be going up on the Aspen Leaf Trail, if he wanted to tag along."

So much for her master plan of escaping the inn today so she could keep her children—and herself—out from underfoot while he was working on the other renovations.

"Are you mad?" Caidy asked.

She forced a smile when she really wanted to sit right down on the straw-covered floor of the stall and cry.

Yes, when she decided to return to Pine Gulch, she had known seeing him again was inevitable. She just hadn't expected to bump into the dratted man every flipping time she turned around.

"Why would I be mad? Your brother and I are friends." Or at least she was working hard at pretending they could be. Anyway, this was his family's ranch. Some part of her had known when she accepted Caidy's invitation to come out for a visit that there was a chance he might be here.

"Oh, good. I was worried things might be weird between the two of you."

But you invited him along anyway? she wanted to ask, but decided that sounded rude. "No. It's perfectly fine," she lied.

"I thought he could lend a hand with the children. He's really patient with them. In fact, he's the one who taught Gabi to ride. Gabi is the daughter of Becca,

Trace's fiancée. Anyway, it's always good to have another experienced rider on hand when you've got kids who haven't been on a horse before."

"Caidy?" he called again.

"Back here, with the puppies," she returned.

A moment later, Taft rounded the corner of a support beam. At the sight of him, everything inside her seemed to shiver.

Okay, really? This was getting ridiculous. She huffed. So far since she had been back in town, she had seen the man in full firefighter turnout gear when he and his crew responded to the inn fire, wearing a low-slung construction belt while he worked on the renovations at the inn, and now he was dressed in worn jeans, cowboy boots and a tan Stetson that made him look dark and dangerous.

Was he purposely trying to look as if he just stepped off every single page of a beefcake calendar?

Taft Bowman—doing his part to fulfill any woman's fantasy.

"Here you are," he said with that irresistible smile.

She couldn't breathe suddenly as the dust motes floating on the air inside the barn seemed to choke her lungs. This wasn't really fair. Why hadn't his hair started to thin a little in the past decade or his gut started to paunch?

He was so blasted gorgeous and she was completely weak around him.

He leaned in to kiss his sister on the cheek. After a little awkward hesitation, much to her dismay he leaned in to kiss her on the cheek, as well. She could do nothing but endure the brush of his mouth on her skin as the familiar scent of him, outdoorsy and male, filled her senses, unleashing another flood of memories.

Before she could make her brain cooperate and think of something to say, her children noticed him for the first time.

"Hi!" Maya beamed with delight.

"Hey, pumpkin. How are things?"

"Look! Puppies!"

She thrust the endlessly patient black puppy at him and Taft graciously accepted the dog. "He's a cute one. What's his name, Caid?"

"Puppy Number Five," she answered. "I don't name them when I sell them as pups without training. I let their new owners do it."

"Look at this one." Alex pushed past his sister to hold up his own chubby little canine friend.

"Nice," Taft said. He knelt right there in the straw and was soon covered in puppies and kids. Even the tired-looking mother dog came over to him for affection.

"Hey, Betsy. How are you holding up with this brood?" he asked, rubbing the dog between the ears and earning a besotted look that Laura found completely exasperating.

"Thanks for coming out," Caidy said.

"Not a problem. I can think of few things I enjoy more than going on a spring ride into the mountains."

"Not too far into the mountains," she assured Laura. "We can't go very far this time of year anyway. Too much snow, at least for a good month or so."

"Aspen Leaf is open, though, isn't it?"

"Yes. Destry and I checked it the other day. She was disappointed to miss the ride today, by the way," Caidy told Laura. "Becca was taking her and Gabi into Idaho Falls for fittings for their flower-girl dresses."

"And you missed out on all that girly fun?" Taft asked, climbing to his feet and coming to stand beside his sister and Laura. Suddenly she felt crowded by his heat and size and…maleness.

"Are you kidding? This will be much more enjoyable. If you haven't heard, Trace is getting hitched in June," she said to Laura.

"To Pine Gulch's newest attorney, if you can believe that," Taft added.

She *had* heard and she was happy for Trace. He had always been very kind to her. Trace, the Pine Gulch police chief, had always struck her as much more serious than Taft, the kind of person who liked to think things through before he spoke.

For being identical twins, Taft and Trace had two very unique personalities, and even though they were closer than most brothers, they had also actively cultivated friendships beyond each other, probably because of their mother's wise influence.

She did find it interesting that both of them had chosen professions in the public-safety sector, although Trace had taken a route through the military to becoming a policeman while Taft had gravitated toward fire safety and becoming a paramedic.

"Why don't we give the kids another few minutes with the puppies?" Caidy said. "I've already saddled a couple of horses I thought would be a good fit."

"Do I need to saddle Joe?"

"Nope. He's ready for you."

Taft grinned. "You mean all I had to do today was show up?"

"That's the story of your life, isn't it?" Caidy said with a disgruntled sort of affection. "If you want to, I'll let you unsaddle everybody when we're done and groom all the horses. Will that make you feel better?"

"Much. Thanks."

The puppy on Maya's lap wriggled through her fingers and waddled over to squat in the straw.

"Look," she exclaimed with an inordinate degree of delight. "Puppy pee!"

Taft chuckled at that. "I think all the puppies are ready for a snack and a nap. Why don't we go see if the horses are ready for us?"

"Yes!" Maya beamed and scampered eagerly toward Taft, where she reached up to grab his hand. After a stunned sort of moment, he smiled at her and folded her hand more securely in his much bigger one.

Alex rose reluctantly and set the puppy he had been playing with down in the straw. "Bye," he whispered, a look of naked longing clear for all to see.

"I hear the kid wants a dog. You know you're going to have to cave, don't you?" Taft spoke in a low voice.

Laura sighed through her own dismay. "You don't think I'm tough enough to resist a six-year-old?"

"I'm not sure a hardened criminal could resist *that* particular six-year-old."

He was right, darn it. She was pretty sure she would have to give in and let her son have a dog. Not a border collie, certainly, because they were active dogs and needed work to do, but she would find something.

As they walked outside the barn toward the horse pasture, she saw Alex's eyes light up at the sight of four horses saddled and waiting. Great. Now he would probably start begging her for a horse, too.

She had to admit, a little burst of excitement kicked through her, too, as they approached the animals. She loved horses and she actually had Taft to thank for that. Unlike many of her schoolmates in the sprawling Pine Gulch school district, which encompassed miles of ranch land, she was a city girl who walked or rode her bike to school instead of taking the bus. Even though she had loved horses from the time she was young—didn't most girls?—her parents had patiently explained they didn't have room for one of their own at their home adjacent to the inn.

She had enjoyed riding with friends who lived outside of town, but had very much considered herself a greenhorn until she became friends with Taft. Even before they started dating, she would often come out to the ranch and ride with him and sometimes Caidy into the mountains.

This would be rather like old times—which, come to think of it, wasn't necessarily a good thing.

Since moving away from Pine Gulch, she hadn't been on a horse one single time, she realized with shock. Even more reason for this little thrum of anticipation.

"Wow, they're really big," Alex said in a soft voice. Maya seemed nervous as well, clinging tightly to Taft's hand.

"Big doesn't have to mean scary," Taft assured him. "These are really gentle horses. None of them will hurt you. I promise. Old Pete, the horse you're going to ride, is so lazy, you'll be lucky to make it around the barn before he decides to stop and take a nap."

Alex giggled but it had a nervous edge to it and Taft gave him a closer look.

"Do you want to meet him?"

Her son toed the dirt with the shiny new cowboy boots she had picked up at the farm-implement store before they drove out to the ranch. "I guess. You sure they don't bite?"

"Some horses do. Not any of the River Bow horses. I swear it."

He picked Maya up in his arms and reached for Alex's hand, leading them both over to the smallest of the horses, a gray with a calm, rather sweet face.

"This is Pete," Taft said. "He's just about the gentlest horse we've ever had here at River Bow. He'll treat you right, kid."

As she watched from the sidelines, the horse bent his head down and lipped Alex's shoulder. Alex froze, eyes wide and slightly terrified, but Taft set a reassuring hand on his other shoulder. "Don't worry. He's just looking for a treat."

"I don't have a treat." Alex's voice quavered a bit. These uncharacteristic moments of fear from her usually bold, mischievous son always seemed to take her by surprise, although she knew they were perfectly normal from a developmental standpoint.

Taft reached into his pocket and pulled out a handful of small red apples. "You're in luck. I always carry a supply of crab apples for old Pete. They're his favorite, probably because I can let him have only a few at a time. It's probably like you eating pizza. A little is great, but too much would make you sick. Same for Pete and crab apples."

"Where on earth do you find crab apples in April?" Laura couldn't resist asking.

"That's my secret."

Caidy snorted. "Not much of a secret," she said. "Every year, my crazy brother gathers up two or three bushels from the tree on the side of the house and stores them down in the root cellar. Nobody else will touch the things—they're too bitter even for pies unless you pour in cup after cup of sugar—but old Pete loves them. Every year Taft puts up a supply so he's got something to bring the old codger."

She shouldn't find it so endearing to imagine him picking crab apples to give to an old, worn-out horse— or to watch his ears turn as red as the apples under his cowboy hat.

He handed one of the pieces of sour fruit to her son and showed him the correct way to feed the horse. Alex held his hand out flat and old Pete lapped it up.

"It tickles like the dog," Alex exclaimed.

"But it doesn't hurt, right?" Taft asked.

The boy shook his head with a grin. "Nope. Just tickles. Hi, Pete."

The horse seemed quite pleased to make his acquaintance, especially after he produced a few more crab apples for the horse, handed to him by Taft.

"Ready to hop up there now?" Taft asked. When the boy nodded, Caidy stepped up with a pair of riding helmets waiting on the fence.

"We're going to swap that fancy cowboy hat for a helmet, okay?"

"I like my cowboy hat, though. I just got it."

"And you can wear it again when we get back. But when you're just learning to ride, wearing a helmet is safer."

"Just like at home when you have to wear your bicycle helmet," Laura told him.

"No helmet, no horse," Taft said sternly.

Her son gave them all a grudging look, but he removed his cowboy hat and handed it to his mother, then allowed Caidy to fasten on the safety helmet. Caidy took Maya from Taft and put one on her, as well, which eased Laura's safety worries considerably.

Finally Taft picked up Alex and hefted him easily into the saddle. The glee on her son's face filled her with a funny mix of happiness and apprehension. He was growing up, embracing risks, and she wasn't sure she was ready for that.

Caidy stepped up to adjust the stirrups to the boy's height. "There you go, cowboy. That should be better."

"What do I do now?" Alex asked with an eager look up into the mountains as if he were ready to go join a posse and hunt for outlaws right this minute.

"Well, the great thing about Pete is how easygoing he is," Taft assured him. "He's happy to just follow along behind the other horses. That's kind of his specialty and what makes him a perfect horse for somebody just beginning. I'll hold his lead line so you won't even have to worry about turning him or making him slow down or anything. Next time you come out to the ranch we'll work on those other things, but this time is just for fun."

Next time? She frowned, annoyed that he would give Alex the impression there would be another time—and that Taft would be part of it, if she ever did bring the kids out to River Bow again. Children didn't forget things like that. Alex would hold him to it and be gravely disappointed if a return trip never materialized.

This was not going at all like she'd planned. She and Caidy were supposed to be taking the children for an easy ride. Instead Taft seemed to have taken over, in typical fashion, while Caidy answered her cell phone a short distance away from the group.

After a moment, Maya grew impatient and tugged on his jeans. "My horse?" she asked, looking around at the animals. She looked so earnest and adorable that it was tough for Laura to stay annoyed at anything.

He smiled down at her with such gentleness that her chest ached. "I was thinking you could just ride with me on my old friend Joe. What do you say, pumpkin? We'll try a pony for you another day, okay?"

She appeared to consider this, looking first at the big black gelding he pointed at, then back at Taft. Finally she gave him that brilliant, wide heartbreaker of a smile. "Okay."

Taft Bowman may have met his match for sheer charm, she thought.

"I guess that just leaves me," she said, eyeing the two remaining horses. Something told her the dappled gray-and-black mare was Caidy's, which left the bay for her.

"Do you need a crab apple to break the ice, too?" Taft asked with a teasing smile so appealing she had to turn away.

"I think I'll manage," she said more tersely than she intended. She modified her tone to be a little warmer. "What's her name?"

"Lacey," he answered.

"Hi, Lacey." She stroked the horse's neck and was rewarded with an equine raspberry sound that made Alex laugh.

"That sounded like her mouth farted!" he exclaimed.

"That's just her way of saying hi." Taft's gaze met hers, laughter brimming in his green eyes, and Laura wanted to sink into those eyes.

Darn the man.

She stiffened her shoulders and resolve and shoved her boot in the stirrup, then swung into the saddle and tried not to groan at the pull of muscles she hadn't used in a long time.

Taft pulled the horse's reins off the tether and handed them to her. Their hands brushed again, a slight touch of skin against skin, and she quickly pulled the reins to the other side and jerked her attention away from her reaction to Taft and back to the thousand-pound animal beneath her.

Oh, she had missed this, she thought, loosely holding the reins and reacquainting herself to the unique feel of being on a horse. She had missed all of it. The stretch of her muscles, the heat of the sun on her bare head, the vast peaks of the Tetons in the distance.

"You ready, sweetie?" he asked Maya, who nodded, although the girl suddenly looked a little shy.

"Everything will be just fine," he assured her. "I won't let go. I promise."

He loosed his horse's reins from the hitch as well as the lead line for old Pete before setting Maya in the saddle. Her daughter looked small and vulnerable at such a height, even under her safety helmet, but she had to trust that Taft would take care of her.

"While I mount up, you hold on right there. It's called the saddle horn. Got it?"

"Got it," she mimicked. "Horn."

"Excellent. Hang on, now. I'll keep one hand on you."

Laura watched anxiously, afraid Maya would slide off at the inevitable jostling of the saddle, but she needn't have worried. He swung effortlessly into the saddle, then scooped an arm around the girl.

"Caid? You coming?" Taft called.

She glanced over and saw Caidy finish her phone conversation and tuck her cell into her pocket, then walk toward them, her features tight with concern. "We've got a problem."

"What's wrong?"

"That was Ridge. A speeder just hit a dog a quarter mile or so from the front ranch gates. Ridge was right behind the idiot and saw the whole thing happen."

"One of yours?" Taft asked.

Her braid swung as she shook her head. "No. I think it's a little stray I've seen around the last few weeks. I've been trying to coax him to come closer to the house but he's pretty skittish. Looks like he's got a broken leg and Ridge isn't sure what to do with him."

"Can't he take him to the vet?"

"He can't reach Doc Harris. I guess he's been trying to find the backup vet but he's in the middle of equine surgery up at Cold Creek Ranch. I should go help. Poor guy."

"Ridge or the stray?"

"Both. Ridge is a little out of his element with dogs. He can handle horses and cattle, but anything smaller than a calf throws him off his game." She paused and sent a guilty look toward Laura. "I'm sorry to do this after I invited you out and all, but do you think you'll be okay with only my brother as a guide while I go help with this injured dog?"

If not for the look in Caidy's eyes, Laura might have thought she had manufactured the whole thing as an elaborate ruse to throw her and Taft together. But either Caidy was an excellent actress or her distress was genuine.

"Of course. Don't worry about a thing. Do you need our help?"

The other woman shook her head again. "I doubt it. To be honest, I'm not sure there's anything *I* can do, but I have to try, right? I'm just sorry to invite you out here and then ditch you."

"No worries. We should be fine. We're not going far, are we?"

Taft shook his head. "Up the hill about a mile. There's a nice place to stop and have the picnic Caidy packed."

She did *not* feel like having a picnic with him but

could think of no graceful way to extricate herself and her children from it, especially when Alex and Maya appeared to be having the time of their lives.

"Thanks for being understanding," Caidy said, with a harried look, unsaddling the other horse at lightning speed. "I'll make it up to you."

"No need," Laura said as her horse took a step or two sideways, anxious to go. "Take care of the stray for us."

"I'll do my best. Maybe I'll try to catch up with you. If I don't make it, though, I'll probably see you later after you come back down."

She glanced up at the sky. "Looks like a few clouds gathering up on the mountain peaks. I hope it doesn't rain on you."

"They're pretty high. We should be fine for a few hours," Taft said. "Good luck with the dog. Shall we, guys?"

Leaving Caidy behind to deal with a crisis felt rude and selfish, but Laura didn't know what else to do. The children would be terribly disappointed if she backed out of the ride, and Caidy was right. What could they do to help her with the injured dog?

She sighed. And of course this also meant she and the children would have to be alone with Taft.

She supposed it was a very good thing Taft had no reason to be romantically interested in her anymore. She had a feeling she would be even more weak than normal on a horseback ride with him into the mountains, especially when she had so many memories of other times and other rides that usually ended with them making out somewhere on the ranch.

"Yes," she finally said. "Let's go."

The sooner they could be on their way, the quicker they could return and she and her children could go back to the way things were before Taft burst so insistently back into her life.

Chapter Seven

With Maya perched in front of him, Taft led the way and held the lead line for Alex's horse while Laura brought up the rear. A light breeze danced in her hair as they traveled through verdant pastureland on their way to a trailhead just above the ranch.

The afternoon seemed eerily familiar, a definite déjà vu moment. It took her a moment to realize why— she used to fantasize about a day exactly like this when she had been young and full of dreams. She used to imagine the two of them spending a lovely spring afternoon together on horseback along with their children, laughing and talking, pausing here and there for some of those kisses she had once been so addicted to.

Okay, they had the horses and the kids here and definitely the lovely spring afternoon, but the rest of it wasn't going to happen. Not on her watch.

She focused on the trail, listening to Alex jabber a mile a minute about everything he saw, from the double-trunked pine tree alongside the trail, to one of Caidy's dogs that had come along with them, to about how much he loved old Pete. The gist, as she fully expected, was that he now wanted a horse *and* a dog of his own.

The air here smelled delicious: sharp, citrusy pine, the tart, evocative scent of sagebrush, woodsy earth and new growth.

She had missed the scent of the mountains. Madrid had its own distinctive smells, flowers and spices and baking bread, but this, this was home.

They rode for perhaps forty minutes until Alex's chatter started to die away. It was hard work staying atop a horse. Even if the rest of him wasn't sore, she imagined his jaw muscles must be aching.

The deceptively easy grade led one to think they weren't gaining much in altitude, but finally they reached a clearing where the pines and aspens opened up and she could look down on the ranch and see its eponymous river bow, a spot where the river's course made a horseshoe bend, almost folding in on itself. The water glimmered in the afternoon sunlight, reflecting the mountains and trees around it.

She admired the sight from atop her horse, grateful that Taft had stopped, then realized he was dismounting with Maya still in his arms.

"I imagine your rear end could use a little rest," he said to Alex, earning a giggle.

"Sí," he said, reverting to the Spanish he sometimes still used. "My bum hurts and I need to pee," he said.

"We can take care of that. Maya, you sit here while I help your brother." He set the girl atop a couch-size boulder, then returned to the horses and lifted Alex down, then turned to Laura again. "What about you? Need a hand?"

"I've got it," she answered, quite certain it wouldn't be a good idea for him to help her dismount.

Her muscles were stiff, even after such a short time on the horse, and she welcomed the chance to stretch her legs a little. "Come on, Alex. I'll take you over to the bushes. Maya, do you need to go?"

She shook her head, busy picking flowers.

"I'll keep an eye on her," Taft said. "Unless you need me on tree duty?"

She shook her head, amused despite herself, at the term. "I've got it."

As she walked away, she didn't want to think about what a good team they made or how very similar this was to those fantasies she used to weave.

Alex thought it was quite a novel thing to take care of his business against a tree and didn't even complain when she whipped the hand sanitizer out of her pocket and made him use it afterward.

The moment they returned to the others, Caidy's dog King brought a stick over and dropped it at Alex's feet, apparently knowing an easy mark when he saw one. Alex picked up the stick and chucked it for the dog as far as his little arm could go and the dog bounded after it while Maya clapped her hands with excitement.

"Me next," she said.

The two were perfectly content to play with the dog and Laura was just as content to lean against a sun-warmed granite boulder and watch them while she listened to a meadowlark's familiar song.

Idaho is a pretty little place. That's what her mother always used to say the birds were trilling. The memory made her smile.

"I can picture you just like that when you were younger. Your hair was longer, but you haven't changed much at all."

He had leaned his hip against the boulder where she sat and her body responded instantly to his proximity, to the familiar scent of him. She edged away so their shoulders wouldn't brush and wondered if he noticed.

"I'm afraid that's where you're wrong. I'm a very different person. Who doesn't change in ten years?"

"Yeah, you're right. I'm not the same man I was a decade ago. I like to think I'm smarter these days about holding on to what's important."

"Do you ride often?" she asked.

A glint in his eye told her he knew very well she didn't want to tug on that particular conversational line, but he went along with the obvious change of topic. "Not as much as I would like. My niece, Destry, loves to ride and now Gabi has caught the bug. As often as they can manage it, they do their best to persuade one of us to take them for a ride. I haven't been up for a few months, though."

He obviously loved his niece. She had already noticed that soft note in his voice when he talked about the girl. She would have expected it. The Bowmans had always been a close, loving family before their parents' brutal murder. She expected they would welcome Becca and her sister into the family's embrace, as well.

"Too busy with your social life?"

The little niggle of envy under her skin turned her tone more caustic than she intended, but he didn't seem offended.

He even chuckled. "Sure. If by *social life* you mean the house I'm building on the edge of town that's filled all my waking hours for the last six months. I haven't had much room for other things."

"You're building it yourself?"

"Most of it. I've had help here and there. Plumbing. HVAC. That sort of thing. I don't have the patience for good drywall work, so I paid somebody else to do that, too. But I've done all the carpentry and most of the electrical. I can give you some good names of subcontractors I trust if you decide to do more on the inn."

"Why a house?"

He appeared to be giving her question serious thought as he watched the children playing with the dog, with the grand sprawl of the ranch below them. "I guess I was tired of throwing away rent money and living in a little apartment where I didn't have room to stretch out. I've had this land for a long time. I don't know. Seemed like it was time."

"You're building a house. That's pretty permanent. Does that mean you're planning to stay in Pine Gulch?"

He shrugged, and despite her efforts to keep as much distance as possible between them, his big shoulder still brushed hers. "Where else would I go? Maybe I should have taken off for somewhere exotic when

I had the chance. What do they pay firefighters in Madrid?"

"I'm afraid I have no idea. I have friends I can ask, though." He would fit in well there, she thought, and the *madrileñas*—the women of Madrid—would go crazy for his green eyes and teasing smile.

Which he utilized to full effect on her now. "That eager to get rid of me?"

She had no answer to that, so she again changed the subject. "Where did you say your house was?"

"A couple of miles from here, near the mouth of Cold Creek Canyon. I've got about five acres there in the trees. Enough room to move over some of my own horses eventually."

He paused, an oddly intent look in his green eyes. "You ought to come see it sometime. I would even let Alex pound a couple of nails if he wanted."

She couldn't afford to spend more time with him, not when he seemed already to be sneaking past all her careful defenses. "I'm sure we've got all the nails Alex could wish to pound at the inn."

"Sure. Yeah. Of course." He nodded, appearing nonchalant, but she had the impression she had hurt him somehow.

She wanted to make it right, tell him she would love to come see his house under construction anytime he wanted them to, but she caught the ridiculous words before she could blurt them out.

Taft picked up an early-spring wildflower—she thought it might be some kind of phlox—and twirled it between his fingers, his gaze on the children playing with the dog. This time he was the one who picked another subject. "How are the kids settling into Pine Gulch?"

"So far they're loving it, especially having their grandmother around."

"What about you?"

She looked out over the ranch and at the mountains in the distance. "It's good. There are a lot of things I love about being home, things I missed more than I realized while I was in Spain. Those mountains, for instance. I had forgotten how truly quiet and peaceful it could be here."

"This is one of my favorite places on the ranch."

"I remember."

Her soft words hung between them and she heartily wished she could yank them back. Tension suddenly seethed between them and she saw that he also remembered the significance of this place.

Right here in this flower-strewn meadow was where they had kissed that first time when he had returned after the dangerous flashover. She had always considered it their place, and every time she came here after that, she remembered the sheer joy bursting through her as he finally—finally!—saw her as more than just his friend.

They had come here often after that. He had proposed, right here, while they were stretched out on a blanket in the meadow grass.

She suddenly knew it was no accident he had stopped the horses here. Anger pumped through her, hot and fierce, that he would dredge up all these hopes and dreams and emotions she had buried after she left Pine Gulch.

With jerky motions, she climbed off the boulder. "We should probably be heading back."

His mouth tightened and he looked as if he wanted to say something else but he seemed to change his mind. "Yeah, you're right. That sky is looking a little ominous."

She looked up to find dark clouds smearing the sky, a perfect match to her mood, as if she had conjured them. "Where did those come from? A minute ago it was perfectly sunny."

"It's springtime in Idaho, where you can enjoy all four seasons in a single afternoon. Caidy warned us about possible rain. I should have been paying more attention. You ready, kids?" he called. "We've got to go."

Alex frowned from where he and Maya were flopped in the dirt petting the dog. "Do we have to?"

"Unless you want to get drenched and have to ride down on a mud slide all the way to the ranch."

"Can we?" Alex asked eagerly.

Taft laughed, although it sounded strained around the edges. "Not this time. It's up to us to make sure the ladies make it back in one piece. Think you're up to it?"

If she hadn't been so annoyed with Taft, she might have laughed at the way Alex puffed out his little chest. "Yes, sir," he answered.

"Up you go, then, son." He lifted the boy up onto the saddle and adjusted his helmet before he turned back to Maya.

"What about you, Maya, my girl? Are you ready?"

Her daughter beamed and scampered toward him.

Watching them all only hardened Laura's intention to fortify her defenses around Taft.

One person in her family needed to resist the man. By the looks of things, she was the only one up for the job.

Maybe.

They nearly made it.

About a quarter mile from the ranch, the clouds finally let loose, unleashing a torrent of rain in one of those spring showers that come on so fast, so cold and merciless that they had no time to really prepare themselves.

By the time they reached the barn, Alex was shivering, Laura's hair was bedraggled and Taft was kicking himself for not hurrying them down the hill a little faster. At least Maya stayed warm and dry, wrapped in the spare raincoat he pulled out of his saddlebag.

He took them straight to the house instead of the barn. After he climbed quickly down from his horse, he set Laura's little girl on the porch, then quickly returned to the horses to help Alex dismount.

"Head on up to the porch with your sister," he ordered. After making sure the boy complied, he reached up without waiting for permission and lifted Laura down, as well. He winced as her slight frame trembled when he set her onto solid ground again.

"I'm sorry," he said. "I should have been paying better attention to the weather. That storm took me by surprise."

Her teeth chattered and her lips had a blue tinge to

them he didn't like at all. "It's okay. My SUV has a good heater. We'll warm up soon enough."

"Forget it. You're not going home in wet clothes. Come inside and we'll find something you and the kids can change into."

"It's fine. We'll be home in fifteen minutes."

"If I let you go home cold and wet, I would never hear the end of it from Caidy. Trust me—the wrath of Caidy is a fearful thing and she would shoot me if I let you get sick. Come on. The horses can wait out here for a minute."

He scooped both kids into his arms, much to their giggly enjoyment, and carried them into the ranch house to cut off any further argument. That they could still laugh under such cold and miserable conditions touched something deep inside him.

He loved these kids already. How had that happened? Alex, with his million questions, Maya with her loving spirit and eager smile. Somehow when he wasn't looking, they had tiptoed straight into his heart and he had a powerful feeling he wasn't going to be able to shoo them out again anytime soon.

He wanted more afternoons like this one, full of fun and laughter and this sense of belonging. Hell, he wasn't picky. He would take mornings or evenings or any time he could have with Laura and her kids.

Yet Laura seemed quite determined to keep adding bricks to the wall between them. Every time he felt as if he was maybe making a little progress, she built up another layer and he didn't know what the hell to do about it.

"Here's the plan," he said when she trailed reluctantly inside after him. "You get the kids out of their wet clothes and wrapped in warm blankets. We've got a gas fireplace in the TV room that will warm you up in a second. Meanwhile, I'll see what I can do about finding something for you to wear."

"This is ridiculous. Honestly, Taft, we can be home and changed into our own clothes in the time it's going to take you to find something here."

He aimed a stern look at her. "Forget it. I'm not letting you leave this ranch until you're dry, and that's the end of it. I'm a paramedic, trained in public safety. How would it look if the Pine Gulch fire chief stood around twiddling his thumbs while his town's newest citizens got hypothermia?"

"Oh, stop exaggerating. We're not going to get hypothermia," she muttered, but she still followed him to the media room of the ranch house, a big, comfortable space with multiple sofas and recliners.

This happened to be one of his favorite rooms at River Bow Ranch, a place where he and his brothers often gathered to watch college football and NBA basketball.

He flipped the switch for the fireplace. The blower immediately came on, throwing welcome heat into the room while he grabbed a couple of blankets from behind one of the leather sofas for the kids.

"Here you go. You guys shuck your duds and wrap up in these blankets."

"Really?" Alex looked wide-eyed. "Can we, Mama?"

"Just for a few minutes, while we throw our clothes in the dryer."

"I'll be back in a second with something of Caidy's for you," he told her.

He headed into his sister's room and quickly found a pair of sweats and a hooded sweatshirt in the immaculately organized walk-in closet.

By the time he returned to the TV room, the children were bundled in blankets and cuddled up on the couch. He set the small pile of clothes on the edge of the sofa.

"Here you go. I know Caidy won't mind if you borrow them. The only thing in this situation that would make her angry would be if I *didn't* give you dry clothes."

Even though her mouth tightened as if she wanted to argue, she only nodded. The wet locks of hair hanging loosely around her face somehow made her even more beautiful to him. She seemed delicate and vulnerable here in the flickering firelight, and he wanted to tuck her up against him and keep her safe forever.

Yeah, he probably should keep that particular desire to himself for the moment.

"Give me a few minutes to take care of the horses and then I can throw your clothes in the dryer."

"I think I can probably manage to find the laundry room by myself," she murmured. "I'll just toss everything in there together after I change."

"Okay. I'll be back in a few minutes."

Caring for the horses took longer than he'd hoped. He was out of practice, he guessed, plus he had three horses to unsaddle.

When he finally finished up in the barn about half an hour later, the rain was still pouring in sheets that slanted sideways from the wind. Harsh, punishing drops cut into him as he headed back up the porch steps and into the entryway.

Caidy wouldn't be happy about him dripping all over her floor but she would probably forgive him, especially because he had done his best to take good care of the horses—and her guests. That would go a long way toward keeping him out of the doghouse.

He headed into Ridge's room to swipe a dry pair of jeans and a soft green henley. After quickly changing, he walked through the house in his bare feet to the TV room to check on Laura and her kids.

When he opened the door, she pressed a finger to her mouth and gestured to one of the sofas. He followed her gaze and found both Alex and Maya asleep, wrapped in blankets and nestled together like Caidy's puppies while a cartoon on the television murmured softly in the background.

"Wow, that was fast," he whispered. "How did *that* happen?"

She rose with a sidelong look at her sleeping children and led the way back into the hall. She had changed into Caidy's clothes, he could see, and pulled her damp hair back into a ponytail. In the too-big hoodie, she looked young and sweet and very much like the girl he had fallen in love with.

"It's been a big afternoon for them, full of much more excitement than they're used to, and Maya, at least, missed her nap. Of course, Alex insists he's too old for a nap, but every once in a while he still falls asleep in front of the TV."

"Yeah, I have that problem, too, sometimes."

"Really? With all that company I've heard you keep? That must be so disappointing for them."

He frowned. "I don't know what you've heard, but the rumors about my social life are greatly exaggerated."

"Are they?"

He didn't want to talk about this now. What he wanted to do was wrap his arms around her, press her up against that wall and kiss her for the next five or six hours. Because he couldn't do that, he figured he should at least try to set the record straight.

"After you broke things off and left for Spain, I… went a little crazy, I'll admit." He had mostly been trying to forget her and the aching emptiness she left behind, but he wasn't quite ready to confess that much to her. A few years later when he found out she had married another man in Madrid and was expecting a baby, he hadn't seen any reason for restraint.

"I did a lot more drinking and partying than I should have. I'm not particularly proud of who I was back then. The thing is, a guy gets a reputation around Pine Gulch and that's how people tend to see him forever. I haven't been that wild in a long time."

"You don't have to explain yourself to me, Taft," she said, rather stiffly.

"I don't want you to think I'm the Cold Creek Casanova people seem to think."

"What does it matter what I think?"

"It matters," he said simply and couldn't resist taking her hand. Her fingers were still cold and he wrapped his bigger hands around hers. "Brrr. Let me warm up your hands. I'm sorry I didn't keep a better eye on the weather. I should have at least provided gloves for you."

"It's fine. I'm not really cold anymore." She met his gaze, then quickly looked away, and her fingers trembled slightly inside his. "Anyway, I don't think the children minded the rain that much. To them, it was all part of the adventure. Alex already told me he pretended he was a Texas marshal trying to track a bad guy. Rain and all, the whole day will be a cherished memory for them both."

Tenderness for this woman—and her children—washed through him just like that rain, carving rivulets and channels through all the places inside him that had been parched for far too long. "You're amazing at that."

A faint blush soaked her cheeks. "At what?"

"Finding the good in every situation. You always used to do that. Somehow I'd forgotten it. If you had a flat tire, you would say you appreciated the chance to slow down for a minute and enjoy your surroundings. If you broke a nail, you would just say you now had a good excuse to give yourself a manicure."

"Annoying, isn't it? How do people stand me?"

Her laugh sounded embarrassed and she tried to tug her hands away, but he held them fast, squeezing her fingers.

"No, I think it's wonderful. I didn't realize until right this moment how much I've missed that about you."

She gazed up at him, her eyes that lovely columbine-blue and her mouth slightly parted. Her fingers trembled again in his and he was aware of the scent of her, flowery and sweet, and of the sudden tension tightening between them.

He wanted to kiss her as he couldn't remember wanting anything in his life, except maybe the first time he had kissed her on the mountainside so many years ago.

If he followed through on the fierce hunger curling through him, she would just think he was being the player the whole town seemed to think he was, taking advantage of a situation just because he could.

Right now she didn't even like him very much. Better to just bide his time, give her a chance to come to know him again and trust him.

Yeah, that would be the wise, cautious thing to do. But as her hands trembled in his, he knew with a grim sort of resignation that he couldn't be wise or cautious. Not when it came to Laura.

As everything inside him tightened with anticipation, he tugged her toward him and lowered his mouth to hers.

Magic. Simply delicious. She had the softest, sweetest mouth and he couldn't believe he had forgotten how perfectly she fit against him.

Oh, he had missed her, missed this.

For about ten seconds, she didn't move anything except her fingers, now curled in his, while his mouth touched and tasted hers. For those ten seconds, he waited for her to push him away. She remained still except for her hands, and then, as if she had come to some internal decision—or maybe just resisted as long as she could—she returned the kiss, her mouth warm and soft and willing.

That was all the signal he needed to deepen the kiss. In an instant, need thundered through him and he released her hands and wrapped his arms around her, pulling her closer, intoxicated by her body pressed against him.

She felt wonderfully familiar but not quite the same, perhaps a little curvier than she'd been back when she had been his. He supposed two children and a decade could do that. He tightened his arms around her, very much appreciating the difference as her curves brushed against his chest.

She made a low sound in her throat and her arms slipped around his neck and he did what he had imagined earlier, pressed her back against the wall.

She kissed him back and he knew he didn't imagine the hitch in her breathing, the rapid heartbeat he could feel beneath his fingers.

This. This was what he wanted. Laura, right here.

All the aimless wandering of the past ten years had finally found a purpose, here in the arms of this woman. He wanted her and her children in his life. No, it was more than just a whim. He *needed* them. He pictured laughter and joy, rides into the mountains, winter nights spent cuddling by the fireplace of the log home he was building.

For her. He was building it for her and he had never realized it until this moment. Every fixture, every detail had been aimed at creating the home they had always talked about building together.

That didn't make sense. It was completely crazy. Yeah, he'd heard her husband died some months back and had grieved for the pain she must have been feeling, but he hadn't even known she was coming home until he showed up to fight the fire at the inn and found her there.

He had thought he was just building the house he wanted, but now he could see just how perfectly she and her children would fit there.

Okay, slow down, Bowman, he told himself. One kiss did not equal happy ever after. He had hurt her deeply by pushing her away so readily after his parents died and it was going take more than just a few heated embraces to work past that.

He didn't care. He had always craved a challenge, whether that was climbing a mountain, kayaking rapids or conquering an out-of-control wildfire. He had been stupid enough to let her go once. He damn well wasn't going to do it again.

She made another low sound in her throat and he remembered how very sexy he used to find those little noises she made. Her tongue slid along his, erotic and inviting, and heat scorched through him, raw and hungry.

He was just trying to figure out how to move this somewhere a little more comfortable than against the wall of the hallway when the sound of the door opening suddenly pierced his subconscious.

A moment later, he heard his sister's voice from the entry at the other side of the house.

"We've got to go look for them." Caidy sounded stressed and almost frantic. "I can't believe Taft didn't make it back before the rain hit. What if something's happened to them?"

"He'll take care of them. Don't worry about it," Ridge replied in that calm way of his.

They would be here any second, he realized. Even though it was just about the toughest thing he'd ever done—besides standing by and letting her walk out of his life ten years ago—he eased away from her.

She looked flustered, pink, aroused. Beautiful.

He cleared his throat. "Laura," he started to say, but whatever thoughts jumbled around in his head didn't make it to words before his siblings walked down the hall and the moment was gone.

"Oh!" Caidy pedaled to a stop when she saw them. Her gaze swiveled between him and Laura and then back to him. Her eyes narrowed and he squirmed at the accusatory look in them, as if he was some sort of feudal lord having his way with the prettiest peasant. Yeah, he had kissed her, but she hadn't exactly put up any objections.

"You made it back safely."

"Yes."

Laura's voice came out husky, thready. She cleared it. Her cheeks were rosy and she refused to meet his gaze. "Yes. Safe but not quite dry. On our way down, we were caught in the first few minutes of the rainstorm. Taft loaned me some of your clothes. I hope you don't mind."

"Oh, of course! You can keep them, for heaven's sake. What about the kids? Are they okay?"

"More than okay." Her smile seemed strained, but he wasn't sure anyone but him could tell. "This was the most exciting thing that has happened to them since we've been back in Pine Gulch—and that's saying something, considering Alex started a fire that had four ladder trucks responding. They were so thrilled by the whole day that they were both exhausted and fell asleep watching cartoons while we have been waiting for our clothes to run through the dryer—which is silly, by the way. We could have been home in fifteen minutes, but Taft wouldn't let us leave in our wet gear."

"Wise man." Ridge spoke up for the first time. His brother gave him a searching look very much like Caidy's before turning back to her. "Great to see you again, Laura."

Ridge stepped forward and pulled her into a hug, and she responded with a warm smile she still hadn't given *Taft*.

"Welcome back to Pine Gulch. How are you settling in?"

"Good. Being home again is...an adventure."

"How's the dog?" Taft asked.

"Lucky. Looks like only a broken leg," Caidy said. "Doc Harris hurried back from a meeting in Pocatello so he could set it. He's keeping him overnight for observation."

"Good man, that Doc Harris."

"I know. I don't know what we're all going to do when he finally retires."

"You'll have to find another vet to keep on speed dial," Taft teased.

Caidy made a face at him, then turned back to Laura. "You and the kids will stay for dinner, won't you? I can throw soup and biscuits on and have it ready in half an hour."

As much as he wanted her to agree, he knew—even

before she said the words—exactly how she would answer.

"Thank you for the invitation, but I'm afraid I'm covering the front-desk shift this evening. I'm sorry. In fact, I should really be going. I'm sure our clothes are dry by now. Perhaps another time?"

"Yes, definitely. Let me go check on your clothes."

"I can do it," Laura protested, but Caidy was faster, probably because she had grown up in a family of boys where you had to move quick if you wanted the last piece of pie or a second helping of potato salad.

Ridge and Laura talked about the inn and her plans for renovating it for the few moments it took for Caidy to return from the laundry room off the kitchen with her arms full of clothing.

"Here you go. Nice and dry."

"Great. I'll go wake up my kids and then we can get out of your way."

"You're not in our way. I promise. I'm so glad you could come out to the ranch. I'm only sorry I wasn't here for the ride, since I was the one who invited you. I'm not usually so rude."

"It wasn't rude," Laura protested. "You were helping a wounded dog. That's more important than a little ride we could have done anytime."

Caidy opened the door to the media room. Laura gave him one more emotion-charged look before following his sister, leaving Taft alone with Ridge.

His brother studied him for a long moment, reminding Taft uncomfortably of their father when he and Trace found themselves in some scrape or other.

"Be careful there, brother," Ridge finally said.

He was thirty-four years old and wasn't at all in the mood for a lecture from an older brother who tended to think he was the boss of the world. "About?"

"I've got eyes. I can tell when a woman's just been kissed."

He was *really* not in the mood to talk about Laura with Ridge. As much as he respected his brother for stepping up and taking care of both Caidy and the ranch after their parents died, Ridge was *not* their father and he didn't have to answer to the man.

"What's your point?" he asked, more belligerently than he probably should have.

Ridge frowned. "You sure you know what you're doing, dredging everything up again with Laura?"

If I figure that out, I'll be sure to let you know. "All I did was take her and her kids for a horseback ride."

Ridge was silent for a long moment. "I don't know what happened between the two of you all those years ago, why you didn't end up walking down the aisle when everybody could tell the two of you were crazy in love."

"Does it matter? It's ancient history."

"Not that ancient. Ten years. And take it from an expert, the choices we make in the past can haunt us for the rest of our lives."

Ridge should definitely know that. He had married a woman completely unsuitable for ranch life who had ended up making everybody around her miserable, too.

"Given your track record with women in the years since," Ridge went on, "I'm willing to bet you're the one who ended things. You didn't waste much time being heartbroken over the end of your engagement."

That shows what you know, he thought. "It was a mutual decision," he lied for the umpteenth time.

"If I remember right, you picked up with that Turner woman just a week or two after Laura left town. And then Sonia Gallegos a few weeks after that."

Yeah, he remembered those bleak days after she left, the gaping emptiness he had tried—and failed—to fill, when he had wanted nothing but to chase after her, drag her home and keep her where she belonged, with him.

"What's your point, Ridge?"

"This goes without saying—"

"Yet you're going to say it anyway."

"Damn straight. Laura isn't one of your Bandito bimbos. She's a decent person with a couple of kids, including one with challenges. Keep in mind she lost her husband recently. The last thing she probably needs is you messing with her head and heart again when she's trying to build a life here."

Like his favorite fishing knife, his brother's words seemed to slice right to the bone.

He wanted her fiercely—but just because he wanted something didn't mean he automatically deserved it. He'd learned that lesson young when his mother used to make him and Trace take out the garbage or change out a load of laundry if they wanted an extra cookie before dinner.

If he wanted another chance with her after the way he had treated her—and damn it, he *did*—he was going to have to earn his way back. He didn't know how yet. He only knew he planned to work like hell to become the kind of man he should have been ten years ago.

Chapter Eight

Laura was going to kill him. Severely.

Five days after going riding with her and her kids above River Bow, Taft set down the big bag of supplies his sister had given him onto the concrete, then shifted the bundle into his left arm so he could use his right arm to wield his key card, the only way after hours to enter the side door of the inn closest to his room.

"Almost there, buddy," he said when the bundle whimpered.

He swiped the card, waiting for the little light to turn green, but it stayed stubbornly red. Too fast? Too slow? He hated these things. He tried it again, but the blasted light still didn't budge off red.

Apparently either the key code wasn't working anymore or his card had somehow become demagnetized.

Shoot. Of all the nights to have trouble, when he literally had his hands full.

"Sorry, buddy. Hang on a bit more and we'll get you settled inside. I promise."

The little brown-and-black corgi-beagle mix perked his ginormous ears at him and gave him a quizzical look.

He tried a couple more times in the vain hope that five or six times was the charm, then gave up, accepting the inevitable trip to the lobby. He glanced at his watch. Eleven thirty-five. The front desk closed at midnight. Barring an unforeseen catastrophe between here and the front door, he should be okay.

He shoved the dog food and mat away from the door in case somebody else had better luck with their key card and needed to get through, then carried the dog around the side of the darkened inn.

The night was cool, as spring nights tended to be in the mountains, and he tucked the little dog under his jacket. The air was sweet with the scent of the flowers Laura had planted and new growth on the trees that lined the Cold Creek here.

On the way, he passed the sign he had noticed before that said Pets Welcome.

Yeah. He really, really hoped they meant it.

The property was quiet, as he might have expected. Judging by the few cars behind him in the parking lot, only about half the rooms at the inn were occupied. He hadn't seen any other guests for a couple of days in his wing of the hotel, which he could only consider a good thing, given the circumstances—though he doubted Laura would agree.

At least his room was close to the side door in case he had to make any emergency trips outside with the injured dog his sister had somehow conned him into babysitting. He had to consider that another thing to add to the win column.

Was Laura working the front desk? She did sometimes, probably after her children were asleep. In the few weeks he'd been living at the inn, most of the time one of the college students Mrs. Pendleton hired was working the front desk on the late shift, usually a flirtatious coed he tried really hard to discourage.

He wasn't sure whether he hoped to find Laura working or would prefer to avoid her a little longer. Not that he'd been avoiding her on purpose. He had been working crazy hours the past few days and hadn't been around the inn much.

He hadn't seen her since the other afternoon, when she had melted in his arms, although she hadn't been far from his mind. Discovering he wanted her back in his life had been more than a little unsettling.

The lobby of the inn had seen major changes in the few weeks since Laura arrived. Through the front windows he could see that the froufrou couches and chairs that used to form a conversation pit of sorts had been replaced by a half-dozen tables and chairs, probably for the breakfast service he'd been hearing about.

Fresh flower arrangements gave a bright, springlike feeling to the place—probably Laura's doing, as well.

When he opened the front door, he immediately spotted a honey-blond head bent over a computer and warmth seeped through him. He had missed her. Silly, when it had been only four days, but there it was.

The dog in his arms whimpered a little. Deciding discretion was the better part of valor and all that, he wrapped his coat a little more snuggly around the dog. No sense riling her before she needed to be riled.

He wasn't technically doing anything wrong—pets *were* welcome after all, at least according to the sign, but somehow he had a feeling normal inn rules didn't apply to him.

He warily approached her and as she sensed him, she looked up from the computer with a ready smile. At the sight of him, her smile slid away and he felt a pang in his gut.

"Oh. Hi."

He shifted Lucky Lou a little lower in his arm. "Uh, hi. Sorry to bug you, but either my key card isn't working or the side door lock is having trouble. I tried to come in that way, but I couldn't get the green light."

"No problem. I can reprogram your card."

Her voice was stiff, formal. Had that stunning kiss ruined even the friendship he had been trying to rekindle?

"I like the furniture," he said.

"Thanks. It was just delivered today. I'm pleased with the colors. We should be ready to start serving breakfast by early next week."

"That will be a nice touch for your guests."

"I think so."

He hated that they had reverted back to polite small talk. They used to share everything with each other and he missed it.

The bundle under his jacket squirmed a little and she eyed him with curiosity.

"Uh, here's my key," he said, handing it over.

She slid it across the little doohickey card reader and handed it back to him. "That should work now, but let me know if you have more trouble."

"Okay. Thanks. Good night."

"Same to you," she answered. He started to turn and leave just as Lou gave a small, polite yip and peeked his head out of the jacket, his mega-size ears cocked with interest.

She blinked, clearly startled. "Is that…"

"Oh, this? Oh. Yeah. You probably need to add him to your list of guests. This is Lucky Lou."

At his newly christened name, the dog peeked all the way out. With those big corgi ears, he looked like a cross between a lemur and some kind of alien creature.

"Oh, he's adorable."

He blinked. Okay, she wasn't yelling. That was a good sign. "Yeah, pretty cute, I guess. Not exactly the most manly of dogs, but he's okay."

"Is this the dog that was hit by a car the other day?"

"This is the one."

To his great surprise, she walked around the side of the lobby desk for a closer look. He obliged by unwrapping the blanket, revealing the cast on the dog's leg.

"Oh, he's darling," she exclaimed and reached out to run a hand down the animal's fur. The dog responded just as Taft wanted to do, by nudging his head closer to her hand. So far, so good. Maybe she wasn't going to kill him after all.

"How is he?" she asked.

"Lucky. Hence the name."

She laughed softly and the sound curled through him, sweet and appealing.

He cleared his throat. "Somehow he came through with just a broken leg. It should heal up in a few weeks, but he needs to be watched closely during that time to make sure he doesn't reinjure himself. He especially can't be around the other dogs at the ranch because they tend to play rough, which poses a bit of a problem."

"What kind of problem?"

"It's a crazy-busy time at the ranch, with spring planting and all, not to mention Trace's wedding. Caidy was looking for somebody who could keep an eye on Lou here and I sort of got roped into it."

He didn't add that his sister basically blackmailed him to take on the responsibility, claiming he owed her this because she told him about the planned horseback ride with Laura and her children in the first place.

"I guess I should ask whether you mind if I keep him here at the inn with me. Most of the time he'll be at the station house or in my truck with me, but he'll be here on the nights I'm not working there."

She cupped the dog's face in her hand. "I would have to be the most hardhearted woman on the planet to say no to that face."

Okay, now he owed his sister big-time. Who knew the way to reach Laura's heart was through an injured mongrel?

As if she suddenly realized how close she was standing, Laura eased away from him. The dog whimpered a little and Taft wanted to join him.

"Our policy does allow for pets," she said. "Usually we charge a hundred-dollar deposit in case of damages, but given the circumstances I'm sure we can waive that."

"I'll try to keep him quiet. He seems to be a well-behaved little guy. Makes me wonder what happened. How he ended up homeless."

"Maybe he ran away."

"Yeah, that's the logical explanation, but he didn't have a collar. Caidy checked with animal control and the vet and everybody else she could think of. Nobody in the county has reported a lost pet matching his description. I wonder if somebody just dropped him off and abandoned him."

"What's going to happen to him? Eventually, I mean, after he heals?" she asked.

"Caidy has a reputation for taking in strays. Her plan is to nurse him back to health and then look for a good placement somewhere for the little guy. Meantime I'm just the dogsitter for a few days."

"And you can take him to the fire station with you?"

"I'm the fire chief, remember? Who's going to tell me I can't?"

She raised an eyebrow. "Oh, I don't know. Maybe the mayor or the city council."

He laughed, trying to imagine any of the local politicians making a big deal about a dog at the fire station. "This is Pine Gulch," he answered. "We're pretty casual about things like that. Anyway, it's only for a few days. We can always call him our unofficial mascot. Lucky Lou, Fire Dog."

The dog's big ears perked forward, as if eager to take on the new challenge.

"You like the sound of that, do you?" He scratched the dog's ears and earned an adoring look from his new best friend. He looked up to find Laura watching him, an arrested look in her eyes. When his gaze collided with hers, she turned a delicate shade of pink and looked away from him.

"Like I said, he doesn't seem to be much of a barker. I'll try to keep him quiet when I'm here so he doesn't disturb the other guests."

"Thank you, I appreciate that. Not that you have that many guests around you to be disturbed."

The discouragement in her voice made him want to hold her close, dog and all, and take away her worries. "Things will pick up come summer," he assured her.

"I hope so. The inn hasn't had the greatest reputation over the years. My mom did her best after my dad died, but I'm afraid things went downhill."

He knew this to be an unfortunate fact. Most people in town steered their relatives and friends to other establishments. A couple new B and Bs had sprung up recently and there were some nice guest ranches in the canyon. None had the advantage of Cold Creek Inn's location and beautiful setting, though, and with Laura spearheading changes, he didn't doubt the inn would be back on track in no time.

"Give it time. You've been home only a few weeks."

She sighed. "I know. But when I think about all the work it's going to require to counteract that reputation, I just want to cry."

He could certainly relate to that. He knew just how

tough it was to convince people to look beyond the past. "If anybody can do it, you're perfect for the job. A degree in hotel management, all those years of international hotel experience. This will be a snap for you."

She gave him a rueful smile—but a smile nonetheless. He drew in a breath, wishing he could set the dog down and pull Laura into his arms instead. He might have considered it, but Lucky made a sound as if warning him against that particular course of action.

"What you need is a dog," he said suddenly. "A *lucky* dog."

"Oh, no, you don't," she exclaimed on a laugh. "Forget that right now, Taft Bowman. I'm too smart to let myself be swayed by an adorable face."

"Mine or the dog's?" he teased.

This smile looked definitely genuine, but she shook her head. "Go to bed, Taft. And take your lucky dog with you."

I'd rather take you.

The words simmered between them, unsaid, but she blushed anyway, as if she sensed the thoughts in his head.

"Good night, then," he said with great reluctance. "I really don't mind paying the security deposit for the dog."

"No need. Consider it my way of helping in Lucky Lou's recovery."

"Thanks, then. I'll try to be sure you don't regret it."

He hitched the dog into a better position, picked

up the key card from the counter and headed down the hall.

He had enough regrets for the both of them.

Her children were in love.

"He's the cutest dog *ever,*" Alex gushed, his dark eyes bright with excitement. "And so nice, too. I petted him and petted him and all he did was lick me."

"Lou tickles," Maya added, her face earnest and sweet.

"Lucky Lou. That's his name, Chief Bowman says."

Alex was perched on the counter, pulling items out of grocery bags, theoretically "helping" her put them away, but mostly just jumbling them up on the counter. Still, she wasn't about to discourage any act of spontaneous help from her children.

"And where was your grandmother while Chief Bowman was letting you play with his dog?" she asked.

The plan had been for Jan to watch the children while Laura went to the grocery store for her mother, but it sounded very much as if they had been wandering through the hotel, bothering Taft.

"She had a phone call in the office. We were coloring at a new table in the lobby, just like Grandma told us to. I promise we didn't go anywhere like upstairs. I was coloring a picture of a horse and Maya was just scribbling. She's not a very good colorer."

"She's working on it, aren't you, *mi hija?*"

Maya giggled at the favorite words and the everyday tension and stress of grocery shopping and counting coupons and loading bags into her car in a rainstorm seemed to fade away.

She was working hard to give her family a good life here. Maybe it wasn't perfect yet, but it was definitely better than what they would have known if she'd stayed in Madrid.

"So you were coloring and…" she prompted.

"And Chief Bowman came in and he was carrying the dog. He has great big ears. They're like donkey ears!"

She had to smile at the exaggeration. The dog had big ears but nothing that unusual for a corgi.

"Really?" she teased. "I've never noticed that about Chief Bowman."

Alex giggled. "The dog, silly! The *dog* has big ears. His name is Lucky Lou and he has a broken leg. Did you know that? He got hit by a car! That's sad, huh?"

"Terribly sad," she agreed.

"Chief Bowman says he has to wear a cast for another week and he can't run around with the other dogs."

"That's too bad."

"I know, huh? He can only sit quiet and be petted, but Chief Bowman says I can do it anytime I want to."

"That's very kind of Chief Bowman," she answered, quite sure her six-year-old probably wouldn't notice the caustic edge to her tone. She knew just what Taft was after—a sucker who would take the dog off his hands.

"He's super nice."

"The dog?"

"No! Chief Bowman! He says I can come visit Lou

whenever I want, and when his cast comes off, I can maybe take him for a walk."

The decided note of hero-worship she heard in Alex's voice greatly worried her. Her son was desperate for a strong male influence in his life. She understood that.

But Taft wasn't going to be staying at the inn forever. Eventually his house would be finished and he would move out, taking his little dog with him.

The thought depressed her, although she knew darn well it was dangerous to allow herself to care what Taft Bowman did.

"And guess what else?" Alex pressed, his tone suddenly cagey.

"What?"

"Chief Bowman said Lucky Lou is going to need a new home once he recovers!"

Oh, here we go, she thought. It didn't take a child-behavior specialist to guess what would be coming next.

Sure enough, Alex tilted his head and gave her a deceptively casual look. "So I was thinking maybe *we* could give him a new home."

You're always thinking, aren't you, kiddo? she thought with resignation, gearing up for the arguments she could sense would follow that declaration.

"He's a super-nice dog and he didn't bark one single time. I know I could take care of him, Mama. I just *know* it."

"I know it," Maya said in stout agreement, although Laura had doubts as to whether her daughter had even been paying attention to the conversation as she played with a stack of plastic cups at the kitchen table.

How was she going to get out of this one without seeming like the meanest mom in the world? The dog *was* adorable. She couldn't deny it. With those big ears and the beagle coloring and his inquisitive little face, he was a definite charmer.

Maybe in a few months she would be in a better position to get a pet, but she was barely holding on here, working eighteen-hour days around caring for her children so she could help her mother rehabilitate this crumbling old inn and bring it back to the graceful accommodations it once had been.

She had to make the inn a success no matter how hard she had to work to do it. She couldn't stomach another failure. First her engagement to Taft, then her marriage. Seeing the inn deteriorate further would be the last straw.

A dog, especially a somewhat fragile one, would complicate *everything*.

"I would really, really love a dog," Alex persisted.

"Dog. Me, too," Maya said.

Drat Taft for placing her in this position. He had to have known her children would come back brimming over with enthusiasm for the dog, pressing her to add him to her family.

Movement outside the kitchen window caught her gaze and through the rain she saw Taft walking toward the little grassy area set aside for dogs. He was wearing a hooded raincoat and carrying an umbrella. At the dog-walking area, he set Lucky Lou down onto the grass and she saw the dog's cast had been wrapped in plastic.

She watched as Taft held the umbrella over the little corgi-beagle mix while the dog took care of business.

The sight of this big, tough firefighter showing such care for a little injured dog touched something deep inside her. Tenderness rippled and swelled inside her and she drew in a sharp breath. She didn't want to let him inside her heart again. She couldn't do it.

This was Taft Bowman. He was a womanizer, just as Javier had been. The more the merrier. That was apparently his mantra when it came to women. She had been through this before and she refused to do it again.

From his vantage point on top of the counter, Alex had a clear view out the window. "See?" he said with a pleading look. "Isn't he a great dog? Chief Bowman says he doesn't even poop in the house or anything."

She sighed and took her son's small hand in hers, trying to soften the difficulty of her words. "Honey, I don't know if this is the best time for us to get a dog. I'm sorry. I can't tell you yes or no right now. I'm going to have to think hard about this before I can make any decision. Don't get your hopes up, okay?"

Even as she said the words, she knew they were useless. By the adoration on his face as he looked out the rain-streaked window at the little dog, she could plainly tell Alex already had his heart set on making a home for Lou.

She supposed things could be worse. The dog was apparently potty-trained, friendly and not likely to grow much bigger. It wasn't as if he was an English sheepdog, the kind of pet who shed enough fur it could be knitted into a sweater.

But then, this was Taft Bowman's specialty, convincing people to do things they otherwise wouldn't even consider.

She was too smart to fall for it all over again. Or at least that's what she told herself.

Chapter Nine

Nearly a week later, Laura spread the new duvet across the bed in the once-fire-damaged room, then stepped back to survey her work.

Not bad, if she did say so herself. She was especially proud of the new walls, which she had painted herself, glazing with a darker earth tone over the tan to create a textured, layered effect, almost like a Tuscan farmhouse.

Hiring someone else to paint would have saved a great deal of time and trouble, of course. The idea of all the rooms yet to paint daunted her, made her back ache just thinking about it. On the other hand, this renovation had been *her* idea to breathe life into the old hotel, and the budget was sparse, even with the in-kind labor Taft had done for them over the past few weeks.

It might take her a month to finish all the other

rooms, but she would still save several thousand dollars that could be put into upgrading the amenities offered by the inn.

She intended to make each room at the inn charming and unique. This was a brilliant start. The room looked warm and inviting and she couldn't wait to start renting it out. She smoothed a hand over the wood trim around the windows, noting the tightness of the joints and the fine grain that showed beautifully through the finish.

"Wow, it looks fantastic in here."

She turned at the voice from the open doorway and found Taft leaning against the doorjamb. He looked tired, she thought, with a day's growth of whiskers on his cheeks and new smudges under his eyes. Not tired, precisely. Weary and worn, as if he had stopped here because he couldn't move another step down the hall toward his own room.

"Amazing the difference a coat of paint and a little love can do, isn't it?" she answered, worried for him.

"Absolutely. I would stay here in a heartbeat."

"You *are* staying here. Okay, not *here* precisely, in this particular room, but at the inn."

"If this room is any indication, the rest of this place will be beautiful by the time you're finished. People will be fighting over themselves to get a room."

"I hope so," she answered with a smile. This was what she wanted. The chance to make this historic property come to life.

"Do you ever sleep?" he asked.

"I could ask the same question. You look tired."

"Yeah, it's been a rough one."

She found the weary darkness in his gaze disconcerting. Taft was teasing and fun, with a smile and a lighthearted comment for everyone. She rarely saw him serious and quiet. "What's happened?"

He sank down onto the new sofa, messing up the throw pillows she had only just arranged. She didn't mind. He looked like a man who needed somewhere comfortable to rest for a moment.

"Car accident on High Creek Road. Idiot tourist took one of those sharp turns up there too fast. The car went off the road and rolled about thirty feet down the slope."

"Is he okay?"

"The driver just had scrapes and bruises and a broken arm." He scratched at a spot at the knee of his jeans. "His ten-year-old kid wasn't so lucky. We did CPR for about twenty minutes while we waited for the medevac helicopter and were able to bring him back. Last I heard, he survived the flight to the children's hospital in Salt Lake City, but he's in for a long, hard fight."

Her heart ached for the child and for his parents. "Oh, no."

"I hate incidents with kids involved." His mouth was tight. "Makes me want to tell every parent I know to hug their children and not let go. You just never know what could happen on any given day. If I didn't know Ridge would shoot me for it, I'd drive over to the ranch and wake up Destry right now, just so I could give her a big hug and tell her I love her."

His love for his niece warmed her heart. He was a man with a huge capacity to love and he must have deep compassion if he could be so upset by the day's events. Hadn't he learned how to keep a safe distance between his emotions and the emergency calls he had to respond to as a firefighter and paramedic?

"I'm sorry you had to go through that today."

He shrugged. "It's part of the job description, I guess. Sometimes I think my life would have been a hell of a lot easier if I'd stuck to raising cattle with Ridge."

These moments always took her by surprise when she realized anew that Taft was more than just the lighthearted, laughing guy he pretended to be. He felt things deeply. She had always known that, she supposed, but it was sometimes easy to forget when he worked so hard to be a charming flirt.

After weighing the wisdom of being in too close proximity to him against her need to offer comfort, she finally sank onto the sofa beside him.

"I'm sure you did everything you could."

"That's what we tell ourselves to help us sleep at night. Yet we always wonder."

He had been driving back to the ranch after being with her that terrible December night his parents were killed, when a terrified Caidy had called 9-1-1, she remembered now. Taft had heard the report go out on the radio in his truck just as he'd been turning into the gates of the ranch and had rushed inside to find his father shot dead and his mother bleeding out on the floor.

Not that he ever talked about this with her, but one of the responding paramedics had told her about finding a blood-covered Taft desperately trying to do CPR on his mother. He wouldn't stop, even after the rescue crews arrived.

His failure to revive his mother had eaten away at him, she was quite certain. If he had arrived five minutes earlier, he might have been able to save her.

She suspected, though of course he blocked this part of his life from her, that some part of him had even blamed Caidy for not calling for rescue earlier. Caidy had been home, as well, and had hidden in a closet in terror for several moments after her parents were shot, not sure whether the thieves—who had come to what they thought was an empty ranch to steal the Bowmans' art collection and been surprised into murder— might still actually be in the house.

After Laura left Pine Gulch, she had wondered if he blocked out his emotions after the murders in an effort to protect himself from that guilt at not being able to do enough to save his parents.

Even though he pretended he was fine, the grief and loss had simmered inside him. If only he had agreed to postpone the wedding, perhaps time would have helped him reach a better place so they could have married without that cloud over them.

None of that mattered now. He was hurting and she was compelled by her very nature to help ease that pain if she could. "What you do is important, Taft, no matter how hard it sometimes must feel. Think of it this way—if not for you and the other rescuers, that boy wouldn't have any chance at all. He wouldn't have made it long enough for the medical helicopter. And he's only one of hundreds, maybe thousands, of people you've helped. You make a real difference here in Pine

Gulch. How many people can say that about their vocation?"

He didn't say anything for a long time and she couldn't read the emotion in his gaze. "There you go again. Always looking for the good in a situation."

"It seems better than focusing on all the misery and despair around me."

"Yeah, but sometimes life sucks and you can't gloss over the smoke damage with a coat of paint and a couple new pictures on the wall."

His words stung more than they should have, piercing unerringly under an old, half-healed scar.

Javier used to call her *dulce y inocente.* Sweet and innocent. He treated her like a silly girl, keeping away all their financial troubles, his difficulties with the hotel, the other women he slept with, as if she were too fragile to deal with the harsh realities of life.

"I'm not a child, Taft. Believe me, I know just how harsh and ugly the world can be. I don't think it makes me silly or naive simply because I prefer to focus on the hope that with a little effort, people can make a difference in each other's lives. We can always make tomorrow a little better than today, can't we? What's the point of life if you focus only on the negative, on what's dark or difficult instead of all the joy waiting to be embraced with each new day?"

She probably sounded like a soppy greeting card, but at that moment she didn't care.

"I never said you were silly." He gave her a probing look that made her flush. "Who did?"

She wanted to ignore the question. What business was it of his? But the old inn was quiet around them and there was an odd sort of intimacy in this pretty, comfortable room.

"My husband. He treated me like I was too delicate to cope with the realities of life. It was one of the many points of contention between us. He wanted to put a nice shiny gloss over everything, pretend all was fine."

He studied her for a long moment, then sighed. "I suppose that's not so different from what I did to you after my parents died."

"Yes," she answered through her surprise that he would actually bring up this subject and admit to his behavior. "If not for our...history, I guess you could say, it might not have bothered me so much when Javier insisted on that shiny gloss. But I had been through it all before. I didn't want to be that fragile child."

Before she realized what he intended, he covered her hand with his there on the sofa between them. His hand was large and warm, his fingers rough from years of both working on the ranch and putting his life on the line to help the residents of Pine Gulch, and for one crazy moment, she wanted to turn her hand over, grab tightly to his strength and never let go.

"I'm so sorry I hurt you, Laura. It was selfish and wrong of me. I should have postponed the wedding until I was in a better place."

"Why didn't you? A few months—that might have made all the difference, Taft."

"Then I would have had to admit I was still struggling to cope, six months later, when I thought I should have been fine and over things. I was a tough firefighter, Laura. I faced wildfires. I ran into burning buildings. I did whatever I had to. I guess I didn't want to show any signs of weakness. It was…tough for me to accept that my parents' murders threw me for a loop, so I pretended I was fine, too selfish and immature a decade ago to consider that you might have been right, that I needed more time."

She closed her eyes, wondering how her life might have been different if she had gone ahead with the wedding, despite all her misgivings. If she had been a little more certain he would come through his anger and grief, if she had married him anyway, perhaps they could have worked through it.

On the other hand, even though she had loved him with all her heart, she would have been miserable in a marriage where he refused to share important pieces of himself with her. They probably would have ended up divorced, hating each other, with a couple of messed-up kids trapped in the middle.

He squeezed her fingers and his gaze met hers. Something glimmered in the depths of those green eyes, emotions she couldn't identify and wasn't sure she wanted to see.

"For the record," he murmured, "nothing was right after you left. It hasn't been right all this time. I've missed you, Laura."

She stared at him, blood suddenly pulsing through her. She didn't want to hear this. All her protective instincts were urging her to jump up from this sofa and escape, but she couldn't seem to make herself move.

"I should have come after you," he said. "But by the time I straightened out my head enough to do it, you were married and expecting a baby and I figured I had lost my chance."

"Taft—" Her voice sounded husky and low and she couldn't seem to collect her thoughts enough to add anything more. It wouldn't have mattered if she had. He didn't give her a chance to say a word before he leaned in, his eyes an intense, rich green, and lowered his mouth to hers.

His mouth was warm and tasted of coffee and something else she couldn't identify. Some part of her knew she should move now, while she still had the will, but she couldn't seem to make any of her limbs cooperate, too lost in the sheer, familiar joy of being in his arms again.

He kissed her softly, not demanding anything, only tasting, savoring, as if her mouth were some sort of rare and precious wine. She was helpless to do anything but try to remember to breathe while her insides twisted and curled with longing.

"I missed you, Laura," he murmured once more, this time against her mouth.

I missed you, too. So much.

The words echoed through her mind but she couldn't say them. Not now. Not yet.

She could do nothing now but soak in the stunning tenderness of his kiss and let it drift around and through her, resurrecting all those feelings she had shoved so deeply down inside her psyche.

Finally, when she couldn't think or feel past the thick flow of emotions, he deepened the kiss. Now. Now was the time she should pull away, before things progressed too far. Her mind knew it, but again, the rest of her was weak and she responded instinctively, as she had done to him so many times before, and pressed her mouth to his.

For long moments, nothing else existed but his strength and his heat, his mouth firm and determined on hers, his arms holding her tightly, his muscles surrounding her. She wasn't sure exactly how he managed it without her realizing, but he shifted and turned her so she was resting back against the armrest of the sofa while he half covered her with his body until she was lost in memories of making love with him, tangled bodies and hearts.

She was still in love with him.

The realization slowly seeped through her consciousness, like water finding a weakness in a seam and dripping through.

She was still in love with Taft and probably had been all this time.

The discovery left her reeling, disoriented. She had loved her husband. *Of course* she had. She never would have married him if she hadn't believed they could make a happy life together. Yes, she had discovered she was unexpectedly pregnant after their brief affair, but she hadn't married him for that, despite the intense pressure he applied to make their relationship legal.

Her love for Javier hadn't been the deep, rich, consuming love she had known with Taft, but she had cared deeply for the man—at first anyway, until his repeated betrayals and his casual attitude about them had eaten away most of her affection for him.

Even so, she realized now, throughout the seven

years of her marriage, some part of her heart had always belonged to Taft.

"We were always so good together. Do you remember?"

The low words thrummed through her and images of exactly how things had been between them flashing through her head. From the very first, they had been perfectly compatible. He had always known just how to kiss, just where to touch.

"Yes, I remember," she said hoarsely. All the passion, all the heat, all the heartbreak. She remembered all of it. The memories of her despair and abject loneliness after leaving Pine Gulch washed over her like a cold surf, dousing her hunger with cruel effectiveness.

She couldn't do this. Not again. Not with Taft.

She might still love him, but that was even more reason she shouldn't be here on this sofa with him with their mouths entwined. She froze, needing distance and space to breathe and think, to remind herself of all the many reasons she couldn't go through this all over again.

"I remember everything," she said coldly. "I'm not the one whose memory might have been blurred by the scores of other people I've been with in the meantime."

He jerked his head back as if she had just slapped him. "I told you, reputation isn't necessarily the truth."

"But it has some basis in truth. You can't deny that."

Even as she snapped the words, she knew this wasn't the core of the problem. She was afraid. That was the bare truth.

She still loved him as much as she ever had, maybe more now that she was coming to know the man he had become over the past decade, but she had given her heart to him once and he had chosen his grief and anger over all she had wanted to give him.

If she only had herself to consider, she might be willing to take the risk. But she had two children to think about. Alex and Maya were already coming to care for Taft. What if he decided he preferred his partying life again and chose that over her and the children? He had done it once before.

Her late husband had done the same thing, chosen his own selfish pursuits over his family, time and again, and she had to remember she wouldn't be the only one devastated if Taft decided he didn't want a family. Her children had already been through the pain of losing their father. At all costs, she had to protect them and the life she was trying to create for them.

"I don't want this. I don't want *you,*" she said firmly, sliding away from him. Despite her resolve, her hands trembled and she shoved them into the pocket of her sweater and drew a deep breath for strength as she stood.

"Like apparently half the women in town, I'm weak when it comes to you, so I'm appealing to your better nature. Don't kiss me again. I mean it, Taft. Leave me and my children alone. We can be polite and friendly when we see each other in town, but I can't go through this again. I won't. The children and I are finally in a good place, somewhere we can be happy and build a future. I can't bear it if you bounce in and out again and break our hearts all over again.

Please, Taft, don't make me beg. Go back to the life you had before and leave us alone."

Her words seemed to gouge and claw at his heart. *I don't want this. I don't want you.*

That was clear enough. He couldn't possibly misunderstand.

The children and I are finally in a good place, somewhere we can be happy and build a future. I can't bear it if you bounce in and out again and break our hearts all over again.

As she had done mere days before their wedding, she had looked at him and found him somehow wanting. Again.

He sucked in a ragged breath, everything inside him achy and sore. This was too much after the misery of the day he had just been through, and left him feeling as battered as if he'd free-floated down several miles of level-five rapids.

In that moment, as he gazed at her standing slim and lovely in this graceful, comfortable room, he realized the truth. He loved her. Laura and her family were his life, his heart. He wanted forever with them—while *she* only wanted him gone.

The loss raced over him like a firestorm, like the sudden flashover he had once experienced as a wildlands firefighter in his early twenties. The pain was just like that fire, hot and raw and wild. He couldn't outrun it; he could only hunker down in his shelter and wait for it to pass over.

He wanted to yell at her—to argue and curse and tell her she was being completely unreasonable. He wasn't the same man he'd been a decade ago. Couldn't she see that? He had been twenty-four years old, just a stupid kid, when she left.

Yeah, it might have taken ten years to figure things out, but now he finally knew what he wanted out of life. He was ready to commit everything to her and her children. He wanted what Trace had found with Becca. Once he had held exactly that gift in his hands and he had let it slip away and the loss of it had never hurt as keenly as it did right in this moment.

What did it matter that he might have changed? She didn't want to risk being hurt again by him and he didn't know how to argue with that.

She was right, he had turned away from the warmth of her love at a time in his life when he had needed it most. He couldn't argue with that and he couldn't change things.

He didn't know how to demonstrate to her that *he* had changed, though, that he needed her now to help him become the kind of man he wanted to be. He would be willing to sacrifice anything to take care of her and her children now, and he had no idea how to prove that to her.

"Laura—" he began, but she shook her head.

"I'm sorry. I'm just…I'm not strong enough to go through this all over again."

The misery in her features broke his heart, especially because he knew he had put it there—now and ten years ago.

She gave him one last searching look, then rushed out of this bright, cheerily decorated room, leaving him alone.

He stood there for a long time in the middle of the floor, trying to absorb the loss of her all over again in this room that now seemed cold and lifeless.

What now? He couldn't stay here at the inn anymore. She obviously didn't want him here and he wasn't sure he could linger on the edges of her life, having to content himself with polite greetings at the front desk and the occasional wave in the hallway.

He had finished the carpentry work Jan asked of him in this room and the other six in this wing that had needed the most repair. Because his house was ready for occupancy, with only a few minor things left to finish, he had no real excuse for hanging around.

She hadn't wanted him here in the first place, had only tolerated his presence because her mother had arranged things. He would give her what she wanted. He needed to move out, although the thought of leaving her and Alex and Maya left him feeling grimly empty.

Losing her ten years ago had devastated him. He had a very strong suspicion the pain of their broken engagement would pale compared to the loss of her now.

Chapter Ten

"So how's the house?"

Taft barely heard his brother's question, too busy watching a little kid about Alex's age eating one of The Gulch's famous hamburgers and chattering away a mile a minute while his parents listened with slightly glazed expressions on their faces.

Tourists, he figured, because he didn't recognize them and he knew most of the people in his town, at least by sight. It was a little early for the full tourism season to hit—still only mid-May, with springtime in full bloom—but maybe they were visiting family for the Mother's Day weekend.

Where were they staying? he wondered. Would it be weird if he dropped over at their booth and casually mentioned Cold Creek Inn and the new breakfast service people were raving about? Yeah, probably. Trace, at least, would never let him hear the end of it.

Anyway, if they asked him about the quality of the food, he would have to admit he had no idea. He had moved out of his room at the inn and into his new house the day before Laura started the breakfast service.

But then, he wasn't going to think about Laura right now. He had already met his self-imposed daily limit about ten minutes after midnight while he had been answering a call for a minor fender bender, a couple of kids who wouldn't be borrowing their dad's new sedan again anytime soon.

And then exceeded his thinking-about-Laura quota about 1:00 a.m. and 2:00 a.m. and 3:00 a.m. And so on and so on.

He was a cute kid, Taft thought now as he watched the kid take a sip of his soda. Not as adorable as Alex, of course, but then, he was a little biased.

"The house?" Trace asked again and Taft had to jerk his attention back to his brother.

"It's been okay," he answered.

"Just okay? Can't you drum up a little more excitement than that? You've been working on this all winter long."

"I'm happy to be done," he answered, not in the mood for an interrogation.

If his brother kept this up, he was going to think twice next time about inviting Trace for a late lunch after a long shift. It had been a crazy idea anyway. He and his twin used to get together often for meals at The Gulch, but since Trace's engagement, his brother's free time away from Becca and Gabi had become sparse, as it should be.

He hadn't been quite ready to go home for a solitary TV dinner after work, so had persuaded Trace to take a break and meet him. They could usually manage to talk enough about the general public safety of Pine Gulch for it to technically be considered a working lunch.

Except now, when the police chief appeared to have other things on his mind.

"I can tell when somebody's lying to me," Trace said with a solemn look. "I'm a trained officer of the law, remember? Besides that, I'm your brother. I know you pretty well after sharing this world for thirty-four years. You're not happy and you haven't been for a couple of weeks now. Even Becca commented on it. What's going on?"

He couldn't very well tell his brother he felt as if Laura had made beef jerky out of his heart. He ached with loneliness for her and for Maya and Alex. Right now, he would give anything to be sitting across the table from them while Maya grinned at him and Alex jabbered his ear off. Even if he could find the words to explain away his lousy mood, he wasn't sure he was ready to share all of that with Trace.

"Maybe I'm tired of the same-old, same-old," he finally said, when Trace continued to give him the Bowman interrogation look: *Talk or you* will *be sorry.*

"I've been doing the same job for nearly six years, with years fighting wildland fires and doing EMT work before I made chief. Maybe it's time for me to think about taking a job somewhere else."

"Where?"

He shrugged. "Don't know. I've had offers here and there. Nevada. Oregon. Alaska, even. A change could be good. Get out of Pine Gulch, you know?"

Trace lifted an eyebrow and looked at him skeptically. "You just finished your new house a week ago. And now you're thinking about leaving it? After all that work you put into it?"

He had come to the grim realization some nights ago during another sleepless episode that it would be torture continuing to live here in Pine Gulch, knowing she was so close but forever out of reach. He missed her. A hundred times a day he wanted to run over to the hotel claiming fire-code enforcement checks or something ridiculous like that just for the chance to see her and the children again.

Being without her had been far easier when she was half a world away in Spain. He was afraid the idea of weeks and months—and possibly *years*—of having her this close but always just out of his reach was more than he could endure.

Maybe it was his turn to leave this time.

"It's just an idea. Something I'm kicking around. I haven't actually *done* anything about it."

Before Trace could answer, Donna Archuleta, who owned The Gulch with her husband, brought over their order.

"Here you go, Chief Bowman." She set down Trace's plate, his favorite roast-beef sandwich with green peppers and onions. "And for the other Chief Bowman," she said in her gravelly ex-smoker voice, delivering Taft's lunch of meat loaf and mashed pota-toes, a particular specialty of Lou's.

"Thanks, Donna."

"You're welcome. How are the wedding plans coming along?" she asked Trace.

His brother scratched his cheek. "Well, I'll admit I'm mostly staying out of it. You'll have to ask Becca that one."

"I would if she would ever come around. I guess now she's opened that fancy attorney-at-law office and doesn't have to wait tables anymore, she must be too busy for us these days."

Trace shook his head with a smile at the cantanker-ous old woman. "I'll bring her and Gabi in for break-fast over the weekend. How would that be?"

"I guess that'll do. You two enjoy your lunch."

She headed away amid the familiar diner sounds of rattling plates and conversation.

He had hoped the distraction would derail Trace's train of thought but apparently not. "If you think taking a job somewhere and moving away from Pine Gulch is what you want and need right now, I say go for it," his brother said, picking up right where he had left off. "You know the family will support you in whatever you decide. We'll miss you but we will all understand."

"Thank you, I appreciate that."

He considered it one of his life's greatest blessings that he had three siblings who loved him and would back him up whenever he needed it.

"We'll understand," Trace repeated. "As long as you

leave for the right reasons. Be damn careful you're running *to* something and not just running away."

Lou must be having an off day. The meat loaf suddenly tasted like fire-extinguisher chemicals. "Running away from *what?*"

Trace took a bite of his sandwich and chewed and swallowed before he answered, leaving Taft plenty of time to squirm under the sympathy in his gaze. "Maybe a certain innkeeper and her kids, who shall remain nameless."

How did his brother do that? He hadn't said a single word to him about Laura, but Trace had guessed the depth of his feelings anyway, maybe before he did. It was one of those weird twin things, he supposed. He had known the first time he met Becca, here in this diner, that Trace was already crazy about her.

The only thing he could do was fake his way out of it. "What? Laura? We were done with each other ten years ago."

"You sure about that?"

He forced a laugh. "Yeah, pretty darn sure. You might have noticed we didn't actually get married a decade ago."

"Yeah, I did pick up on that. I'm a fairly observant guy." Trace gave him a probing look. "And speaking of observant, I've also got an active network of confidential informants. Word is you haven't been to the Bandito for the greater part of a month, which coincidentally happens to be right around the time Laura Santiago showed up back in town with her kids."

"Checking up on me?"

"Nope. More like vetting questions from certain

segments of the female society in Pine Gulch about where the hell you've been lately. Inquiring minds and all that."

He took a forkful of mashed potatoes, but found them every bit as unappealing as the meat loaf. "I've been busy."

"So I hear. Working on renovations at the inn, from what I understand."

"Not anymore. That's done now."

He had no more excuses to hang around Cold Creek Inn. No more reason to help Alex learn how to use power tools, to listen to Maya jabber at him, half in a language he didn't understand, or to watch Laura make the inn blossom as she had dreamed about doing most of her life.

Yeah, he wasn't sure he could stick around town and watch as Laura settled happily into Pine Gulch, working on the inn, making friends, moving on.

All without him.

"When I heard from Caidy that you'd moved into the inn and were helping Laura and her mother with some carpentry work, I thought for sure you and she were starting something up again. Guess I was wrong, huh?"

Another reason he should leave town. His family and half the town were probably watching and waiting for just that, to see if the two of them would pick up where they left off a decade and an almost-wedding later.

"Laura isn't interested in rekindling anything. Give her a break, Trace. I mean, it hasn't even been a year since she lost her husband. She and the kids are trying to settle into Pine Gulch again. She's got big plans for the inn, and right now that and her children are where her focus needs to be."

Some of his despair, the things he thought he had been so careful not to say, must have filtered through his voice anyway. His brother studied him for a long moment, compassion in his green eyes Taft didn't want to see.

He opened his mouth to deflect that terrible sympathy with some kind of stupid joke, but before he could come up with one, his radio and Trace's both squawked at the same moment.

"All officers in the vicinity. I've got a report of a Ten Fifty-Seven. Two missing juveniles in the area of Cold Creek Inn. Possible drowning."

Everything inside him froze to ice, crackly and fragile.

Missing juveniles. Cold Creek Inn. Possible drowning.

Alex and Maya.

He didn't know how he knew so completely, but his heart cramped with agony and bile rose in his throat for a split second before he shoved everything aside. Not now. There would be time later, but right now he needed to focus on what was important.

He and Trace didn't even look at each other. They both raced out of the restaurant to their vehicles parked beside each other and squealed out of the parking lot.

He picked up his radio. "Maria, this is Fire Chief Bowman. I want every single damn man on the fire department to start combing the river."

"Yes, sir," she answered.

His heart pounding in his chest, he sped through the short three blocks to Cold Creek Inn, every light flashing and every siren blaring away as he drove with a cold ball of dread in his gut. He couldn't go through this. Not with her. Everything inside him wanted to run away from what he knew would be deep, wrenching pain, but he forced himself to push it all out of his head.

He beat Trace to the scene by a heartbeat and didn't even bother to turn off his truck, just raced to where he saw a group of people standing beside the fast-moving creek.

Laura was being restrained by two people, her mother and a stranger, he realized. She was crying and fighting them in a wild effort to jump into the water herself.

"Laura, what's happened?"

She gazed blankly at him for a moment, her eyes wide and shocky, then her features collapsed with raw relief.

"Taft, my children," she sobbed and it was the most heartrending sound he had ever heard. "I have to go after them. Why won't anyone let me go after them?"

Jan, still holding her, was also in tears and appeared even more hysterical, her face blotchy and red. He wouldn't be able to get much information out of either of them.

Beyond them, he could see the water running fast and high and Lucky Lou running back and forth along the bank, barking frantically.

"Laura, honey, I need you to calm down for just a moment." While everything inside him was screaming urgency, he forced himself to use a soothing, measured tone, aware it might be his only chance to get through to her.

"Please, sweetheart, this is important. Why do you think they're in the river? What happened?"

She inhaled a ragged breath, visibly struggling to calm herself down to answer his question—and he had never loved her more than in that single moment of stark courage.

"They were just here. Right here. Playing with Lucky. They know they're not to go near the creek. I've told them a hundred times. I was out here with them, planting flowers, and kept my eye on them the whole time. I walked around the corner of the inn for another flat and was gone maybe thirty seconds. That's all. When I came back Lucky was running along the bank and they were g-gone." She said the last word on a wailing sob that made everything inside him ache.

"How long ago?"

The stranger, who must have restrained her from jumping in after them, spoke. "Three minutes. Maybe four. Not long. I pulled into the parking lot just in time to see her running down the bank screaming something about her kids. I stopped her from jumping in after them and called 9-1-1. I don't know if that was right."

He would shake the guy's hand later and pay for his whole damn stay, but right now he didn't have even a second to spare.

"You did exactly right. Laura, stay here. Promise me," he ordered. "You won't find them by jumping in and you'll just complicate everything. The water is moving too fast for you to catch up. Stay here and I will bring them back to you. Promise me."

Her eyes were filled with a terrified anguish. He wanted to comfort her, but damn it, he didn't have time.

"Promise me," he ordered again.

She sagged against the stranger and Jan and nodded, then collapsed to her knees in the dirt, holding on to her mother.

He raced back to his truck, shouting orders into his radio the whole time as he set up a search perimeter and called in the technical rescue team. Even as one part of his mind was busy dealing with the logistics of the search and setting up his second in command to run the grid, the other part was gauging the depth of the water, velocity of the current, the creek's route.

Given that the incident happened five minutes ago now, he tried to calculate how far the children might have floated. It was all guesswork without a meter to give him exact stream flow, but he had lived along Cold Creek all his life and knew its moods and its whims. He and Trace and their friends used to spend summers fishing for native rainbows, and as he grew older, he had kayaked the waters innumerable times, even during high runoff.

Something urged him to head toward Saddleback Road. Inspiration? Some kind of guardian angel? Just a semi-educated guess? He didn't know, but a picture formed itself clearly in his head, of a certain spot where the creek slowed slightly at another natural bow and split into two channels before rejoining. Somehow he knew *that* was the spot where he needed to be right now.

He could be totally off the mark but he could only hope and pray he wasn't.

"Battalion Twenty, what's your status?" he heard over the radio. Trace.

"Almost to Saddleback," he said, his voice hoarse. "I'm starting here. Send a team to the road a quarter mile past that. What is that? Barrelwood?"

"Copy. Don't be stupid, Chief."

One of the hazards of working with his brother—but he didn't care about that now, when he had reached the spot that seemed imprinted in his mind, for all those reasons he couldn't have logically explained.

He jerked the wheel to the side of the road and jumped out, stopping only long enough to grab the water-rescue line in its throw bag in one of the compartments in the back of his truck. He raced to the water's edge, scanning up and down for any sign of movement. This time of year, mid-May, the runoff was fast and cold coming out of the mountains, but he thanked God the peak flow, when it was a churning, furious mess, was still another few weeks away as the weather warmed further.

Had he overshot them or had they already moved past him? Damn it, he had no way of knowing. Go down or up? He screwed his eyes shut and again that picture formed in his head of the side channel that was upstream about twenty yards. He was crazy to follow such a vague impression but it was all he had right now.

He raced up the bank, listening to the reports of the search on his radio as he ran.

Finally he saw the marshy island in the middle of the two channels. A couple of sturdy pine trees grew there, blocking a good part of his view, but he strained his eyes.

There!

Was that a flash of pink?

He moved a little farther upstream for a different vantage point. The instant he could see around the pines, everything inside him turned to that crackly ice again.

Two small dark heads bobbed and jerked, snagged in the deadfall of a tree that was half-submerged in the water. The tree was caught between two boulders in the side channel. From here, he couldn't tell if the kids were actually actively holding on or had just been caught there by the current.

He grabbed his radio, talking as he moved as close as he could. "Battalion Twenty. I've got a sighting twenty yards east of where my truck is parked on Saddleback Road. I need the tech team and Ambulance Thirty-Six here now."

He knew, even as he issued the order, that no way in hell was he going to stand here and do nothing during the ten minutes or so it might take to assemble the team and get them here. Ten minutes was the difference between life and death. Anything could happen in those ten minutes. He didn't know if the children were breathing—and didn't even want to think about any other alternative—but if they weren't, ten minutes could be critical to starting CPR.

Besides that, the water could be a capricious, vengeful thing. The relentless current could tug them farther downstream and away from him. He wasn't about to take that chance.

This was totally against protocol, everything he had trained his own people *not* to do. Single-man water rescues were potentially fatal and significantly increased the dangers for everybody concerned.

Screw protocol.

He needed to reach Laura's children. Now.

This would be much more comfortable in a wet suit but he wasn't about to take the time to pull his on. He raced upstream another ten yards to a small bridge formed by another fallen tree. On the other side of the creek, the children were only a dozen feet away. He called out and thought he saw one of the dark heads move.

"Alex! Maya! Can you hear me?"

He thought he saw the head move again but he couldn't be sure. No way could they catch the throw bag. He was going to have to go after them, which he had known from the moment he spotted that flash of pink.

If he calculated just right and entered at the correct place upstream, the current would float him right to them, but he would have to aim just right so the first boulder blocked his movement and his weight didn't dislodge the logjam, sending the children farther downstream.

He knew the swift-water safety algorithm. Talk. Reach. Wade. Throw. Helo. Go. Row. Tow. The only thing he could do here was reach them and get them the hell out.

He tied the rescue rope around the sturdy trunk of a cottonwood, then around his waist, then plunged into the water that came up to his chest. The icy water was agony and he felt his muscles cramp instantly, but he waded his way toward the deadfall, fighting the current as hard as he could. It was useless. After only a few steps, the rushing water swept his feet out from under him, as he expected.

It took every ounce of strength he could muster to keep his feet pointed downstream so they could take the brunt of any impact with any boulders or snags in the water. The last thing he needed here was a head injury.

He must have misjudged the current because he ended up slightly to the left of the boulder. He jammed his numb feet on the second boulder to stop his momentum. A branch of the dead tree gouged the skin of his forehead like a bony claw, but he ignored it, fighting his way hand over hand toward the children, praying the whole time he wouldn't dislodge the trunk.

"Alex, Maya. It's Chief Bowman. Come on, you guys." He kept up a nonstop dialogue with them but was grimly aware that only Alex stirred. The boy opened one eye as Taft approached, then closed it again, looking as if he were utterly exhausted.

The boy's arm was around his sister, but Maya was facedown in the water. He used all his strength to fight the current as he turned her and his gut clenched when he saw her eyes staring blankly and her sweet features still and lifeless.

He gave her a quick rescue breath. She didn't respond, but he kept up the rescue breaths to her and Alex while he worked as quickly as he could, tying them both to him with hands that he could barely feel, wondering as he worked and breathed for all three of them how much time had passed and what the hell was taking his tech rescue crew so long.

This was going to be the toughest part, getting them all out of the water safely, but with sheer muscle, determination—and probably some help from those guardian angels he was quite certain had to be looking after these two kids—he fought the current and began pulling himself hand over hand along the tree trunk, wet and slippery with moss and algae, pausing every ten seconds to give them both rudimentary rescue breaths.

Just as he reached the bank, completely exhausted by the effort of fighting the current, he heard shouts and cries and felt arms lifting him out and untying the kids.

"Chief! How the hell did you find them clear over here?" Luke Orosco, his second in command, looked stunned as he took in the scene.

He had no idea how to explain the process that had led him here. Miracle or intuition, it didn't matter, not when both children were now unresponsive, although it appeared Alex was at least breathing on his own.

Satisfied that his crew was working with Alex, he immediately turned to the boy's sister and took command. He was the only trained paramedic in this group, though everyone else had basic EMT training. "Maya? Come on, Maya, honey. You've got to breathe, sweetheart."

He bent over the girl and turned her into recovery position, on her side, nearly on her stomach, her knee up to drain as much water from her lungs as he could. He could hear Alex coughing up water, but Maya remained still.

"Come on, Maya."

He turned her and started doing CPR, forcing himself to lock away his emotions, the knowledge that Laura would be destroyed if he couldn't bring back her daughter. He continued, shaking off other crew members who wanted to take over.

Some part of him was afraid all this work was for nothing—she had been in the water too long—but then, when despair began to grip him colder than the water, he felt something change. A stirring, a movement, a heartbeat. And then she gave a choking cough and he turned her to her side just in time as she vomited what seemed like gallons of Cold Creek all over the place.

Pink color began to spread through her, another miracle, then she gave a hoarse, raspy cry. He turned her again to let more water drain, then wrapped her in a blanket one of his crew handed over.

"Oxygen," he called. Maya continued to cry softly and he couldn't bring himself to let her go.

"Good job, Chief!"

He was vaguely aware of the guys clapping him and themselves on the back and the air of exultation that always followed a successful rescue, but right now he couldn't focus on anything but Maya.

"You ready for us to load her up?" Ron asked.

He didn't want to let her go, but he knew she needed

more than the triage treatment they could offer here. There was still a chance she had been without oxygen long enough for brain damage, but he had to hope the cold water might help ease that possibility.

"Yeah, we'd better get her into the ambulance," he answered. When the EMTs loaded her onto the stretcher, he finally turned to find Alex being loaded onto another stretcher nearby. The boy was conscious and watching the activity around him. When Taft approached, his mouth twisted into a weary smile.

"Chief." The kid's voice sounded hoarse, raw. "You saved us. I knew you would."

He gripped the boy's hand, humbled and overwhelmed at that steady trust. "What happened, Alex? You know you're not supposed to be near the water."

"I know. We always stay away from it. *Always.* But Lucky ran that way and Maya followed him. I chased after her to take her back to Mama and she thought it was a game. She laughed and ran and then slipped and went in the creek. I didn't know what to do. I thought...I thought I could get her. I had swimming lessons last year. But the water was so *fast.*"

The boy started to cry and he gathered him up there on the stretcher as he had done Maya. What a great kid he was, desperately trying to protect his little sister. Taft felt tears threaten, too, from emotion or delayed reaction, he didn't know, but he was deeply grateful for any guardian angels who had been on his rescue squad for this one.

"You're safe now. You'll be okay."

"Is Maya gonna be okay?" Alex asked.

He still wasn't sure he knew the answer to that. "My

best guys are just about to put her in the ambulance.
You get to take a ride, too."

Before Alex could respond to that, Taft saw a Pine
Gulch P.D. SUV pull up to the scene. His brother's vehicle. The thought barely registered before the passen-
ger door was shoved open and a figure climbed out.

Laura.

She stood outside the patrol vehicle for just a
moment as if not quite believing this could be real and
then she rushed toward them. In a second she scooped
Alex into her arms and hugged him.

"Oh, baby. Sweetheart," she sobbed. "You're okay.
You're really okay? And Maya?" Still carrying Alex,
she rushed over to Maya and pulled her into her other
arm.

"I'm sorry, ma'am, but we need to transport both of
the children to the clinic in town." Ron looked compassionate but determined. "They're in shock and need to
be treated for possible hypothermia."

"Oh. Of course." Her strained features paled a little
at this further evidence that while the children were
out of the water, they still required treatment.

"They're going to be okay, Laura," Taft said. He
hoped anyway, though he knew Maya wasn't out of
the woods.

She glanced over at him and seemed to have noticed
him for the first time. "You're bleeding."

Was he? Probably from that branch that had caught
him just as he was reaching the children. He hadn't
even noticed it in the rush of adrenaline but now he
could feel the sting. "Just a little cut. No big deal."

"And you're soaking wet."

"Chief Bowman pulled us out of the water, Mama," Alex announced, his voice still hoarse. "He tied a rope to a tree and jumped in and got us both. That's what *I* should have done to get Maya."

She gazed at her son and then at Taft, then at the roaring current and the rope still tied to the tree.

"You saved them."

"I told you I would find them."

"You did."

He flushed, embarrassed by the shock and gratitude in her eyes. Did she really think he would let the kids drown? He loved them. He would have gone after them no matter what the circumstances.

"And broke about a dozen rules for safe rescue in the process," Luke Orosco chimed in, and he wanted to pound the guy for opening his big mouth.

"I don't care," she said. "Oh, thank you. Taft, thank you!"

She grabbed him and hugged him, Alex still in her arms, and his arms came around her with a deep shudder. He couldn't bear thinking about what might have happened. If he had overshot the river and missed them. If he hadn't been so close, just at The Gulch, when the call came in. A hundred small tender mercies had combined to make this moment possible.

Finally Luke cleared his throat. "Uh, Doc Dalton is waiting for us at the clinic."

She stepped away from him and he saw her eyes were bright with tears, her cheeks flushed. "Yes, we should go."

"We should be able to take you and both kids all in one ambulance," Luke offered.

"Perfect. Thank you so much."

She didn't look at him again as the crews loaded the two kids into their biggest ambulance. There wasn't room for him in there, although he supposed as battalion chief he could have pulled rank and insisted he wanted to be one of the EMTs assisting them on the way to the hospital.

But Laura and her children were a family unit that didn't have room for him. She had made that plain enough. He would have to remain forever on the outside of their lives. That was the way Laura wanted things and he didn't know how to change her mind.

He watched the doors close on the ambulance with finality, then Cody Shepherd climb behind the wheel and pull away from the scene. As he watched them drive away, he was vaguely aware of Trace moving to stand beside him. His brother placed a hand on his shoulder, offering understanding without words.

Another one of those twin things, he supposed. Trace must have picked up on his yearning as he watched the family he wanted drive away from him.

"Good save," Trace said quietly. "But it's a damn miracle all three of you didn't go under."

"I know." The adrenaline rush of the rescue was fading fast, leaving him battered and embarrassingly weak-kneed.

"For the record, you ever pull a stunt like that again, trying a single-man water rescue, Ridge and I will drag what's left of you behind one of the River Bow horses."

"What choice did I have? I knew the deadfall wasn't going to hold them for long, the way the current was pushing at them. Any minute, they were going to break free and float downstream and I wouldn't have had a second chance. Think if it was Destry or Gabi out there. You would have done the same thing."

Taft was silent for a moment. "Yeah, probably. That still doesn't make it right."

Terry McNeil, one of his more seasoned EMTs, approached the two of them with his emergency kit. "Chief, your turn."

He probably needed a stitch or two, judging by the amount of blood, but he wasn't in the mood to go to the clinic and face Laura again, to be reminded once more of everything he couldn't have. "I'll take care of it myself."

"You sure? That cut looks deep."

He gave Terry a long look, not saying anything, and the guy finally shrugged. "Your call. You'll need to clean it well. Who knows what kind of bacteria is floating in that water."

"I'm heading home to change anyway. I'll clean it up there."

He knew he should be jubilant after a successful rescue. Some part of him was, of course. The alternative didn't bear thinking about, but he was also crashing now after an all-nighter at the fire station combined with exhaustion from the rescue. Right now, all he wanted to do was go home and sleep.

"Don't be an idiot," Terry advised him, an echo of what his brother had said earlier.

He wanted to tell both of them it was too late for that. He had been nothing short of an idiot ten years ago when he let Laura walk away from him. Once, he had held happiness in his hands and had blown it away just like those cottonwood puffs floating on the breeze.

She might be back but she wouldn't ever be his, and the pain of that hurt far worse than being battered by the boulders and snags and raging current of Cold Creek.

Chapter Eleven

So close. She had been a heartbeat away from losing everything.

Hours after the miracle of her children's rescue, Laura still felt jittery, her insides achy and tight with reaction. She couldn't bear to contemplate what might have been.

If not for Taft and his insane heroics, she might have been preparing for two funerals right now instead of sitting at the side of her bed, watching her children sleep. Maya was sucking her thumb, something she hadn't done in a long time, while Alex slept with his arm around his beloved dog, who slept on his side with his short little legs sticking straight out.

So much for her one hard-and-fast rule when she had given in to Alex's determined campaign and allowed the adoption of Lucky Lou.

No dogs on the bed, she had told her son firmly, again and again, but she decided this was a night that warranted exceptions.

She hadn't wanted to let either of them out of her sight, even at bedtime. Because she couldn't watch them both in their separate beds, she had decided to lump everyone together in here, just this once. She wasn't sure where she would sleep, perhaps stretched across the foot of the bed, but she knew sleep would be a long time coming anyway.

She should be exhausted. The day had been draining. Even after the rescue, they had spent several hours at the clinic, until Dr. Dalton and his wife, Maggie, had been confident the children appeared healthy enough to return home.

Dr. Dalton had actually wanted to send them to the hospital in Idaho Falls for overnight observation, but after a few hours, Maya was bouncing around the bed in her room like a wild monkey and Alex had been jabbering a mile a minute with his still-raspy voice.

"You can take them home," Dr. Dalton had reluctantly agreed, his handsome features concerned but kind, "as long as they remain under strict observation. Call me at once if you notice any change in breathing pattern or behavior."

She was so grateful to have her children with her safe and sound that she would have agreed to anything by that point. Every time she thought about what might have happened if Taft hadn't been able to find the children, her stomach rolled with remembered fear and she had to fold her arms around it and huddle for a few moments until she regained control.

She would never forget that moment she climbed out of his brother's patrol vehicle and had seen Taft there, bloodied and soaking wet, holding her son close. Something significant had shifted inside her in that moment, something so profound and vital that she shied away from examining it yet.

She was almost relieved when a crack of light through the doorway heralded her mother's approach. Jan pushed the door open and joined her beside the bed. Her mother looked older than she had that morning, Laura reflected. The lines fanning out from her eyes and bracketing her mouth seemed to have been etched a little deeper by the events of the day.

"They look so peaceful when they're sleeping, don't they?" Jan murmured, gazing down at her only grandchildren.

Laura was suddenly awash with love for her mother, as well. Jan had been a source of steady support during her marriage. Even though Laura hadn't revealed any of the tumult of living with Javier—she still couldn't—she had always known she could call or email her mother and her spirits would lift.

Her mother hadn't had an easy life. She had suffered three miscarriages before Laura was born and two after. When Laura was a teenager, she had often felt the pressure of that keenly, knowing she was the only one of six potential siblings who had survived. She could only hope she was the kind of daughter her mother wanted.

"They do look peaceful," she finally answered, pitching her voice low so she didn't wake the children, although she had a feeling even the high-school marching band would have a tough time rousing them after their exhausting day. "Hard to believe, looking at them now, what kind of trouble they can get into during daylight hours, isn't it?"

"I should have fenced off the river a long time ago." Weary guilt dragged down the edges of her mother's mouth.

Laura shook her head. "Mom, none of this was your fault. I should have remembered not to take my eyes off them for a second. They're just too good at finding their way to trouble."

"If Taft hadn't been there…"

She reached out and squeezed her mother's hand, still strong and capable at seventy. "I know. But he *was* there." And showed incredible bravery to climb into the water by himself instead of waiting for a support team. The EMTs couldn't seem to stop talking about the rescue during the ambulance ride to the clinic.

"Everyone is okay," she went on. "No lasting effects, Dr. Dalton said, except possibly intestinal bugs from swallowing all that creek water. We'll have to keep an eye out for stomachaches, that sort of thing."

"That's a small thing. They're here. That's all that matters." Her mother gazed at the children for a long moment, then back at Laura, her eyes troubled. "You're probably wondering why you ever came home. With all the trouble we've had since you arrived—fires and near-drownings and everything—I bet you're thinking you would have been better off to have stayed in Madrid."

"I wouldn't want to be anywhere else right now,

Mom. I still think coming home was the right thing for us."

"Even though it's meant you've had to deal with Taft again?"

She squirmed under her mother's probing look. "Why should that bother me?"

"I don't know. Your history together, I guess."

"That history didn't seem to stop you from inviting the man to live at the inn for weeks!"

"Don't think I didn't notice during that time how you went out of your way to avoid him whenever you could. You told me things ended amicably between you, but I'm not so sure about that. You still have feelings for him, don't you?"

She started to give her standard answer. *The past was a long time ago. We're different people now and have both moved on.*

Perhaps because the day had been so very monumental, so very profound, she couldn't bring herself to lie to her mother.

"Yes," she murmured. "I've loved him since I was a silly girl. It's hard to shut that off."

"Why do you need to? That man still cares about you, my dear. I could tell that first day when he came to talk to me about helping with the inn renovations. He jumped into the river and risked his life to save your children. That ought to tell you something about the depth of his feelings."

She thought of the dozens of reasons she had employed to convince herself not to let Taft into her life again. None of them seemed very important right now—or anything she wanted to share with her mother. "It's complicated."

"Life is complicated, honey, and hard and stressful and exhausting. And *wonderful*. More so if you have a good man to share it with."

Laura thought of her father, one of the best men she had ever known. He had been kind and compassionate, funny and generous. The kind of man who often opened the doors of his inn for a pittance—or sometimes nothing—to people who had nowhere else to go.

In that moment, she would have given anything if he could be there with them, watching over her children with them.

Perhaps he had been, she thought with a little shiver. By rights, her children should have died today in the swollen waters of Cold Creek. That they survived was nothing short of a miracle and she had to think they had help somehow.

She missed her father deeply in that moment. He had loved Taft and had considered him the son he had always wanted. Both of her parents had been crushed by the end of her engagement, but her father had never pressed her to know the reasons.

"While you were busy at the clinic this afternoon," Jan said after a moment, "I was feeling restless and at loose ends and needed to stay busy while I waited for you. I had to do something so I made a caramel-apple pie. You might not remember but that was always Taft's favorite."

He did have a sweet tooth for pastries, she remembered.

"It's small enough payment for giving me back my

grandchildren, but it will have to do for now, until I can think of something better. I was just about to take it to him…unless you would like to."

Laura gazed at her sleeping children and then at her mother, who was trying her best to be casual and nonchalant instead of eagerly coy. She knew just what Jan was trying to do—push her and Taft back together, which was probably exactly the reason she agreed to let him move into the inn under the guise of trading carpentry work for a room.

Jan was sneaky that way. Laura couldn't guess at her motives—perhaps her mother was looking for any way she could to bind Laura and her children to Pine Gulch. Or perhaps she was matchmaking simply because she had guessed, despite Laura's attempts to put on a bright facade, that her marriage had not been a happy one and she wanted to see a different future for her daughter.

Or perhaps Jan simply adored Taft, because most mothers did.

Whatever the reason, Laura had a pivotal decision to make: Take the pie to him herself as a small token of their vast gratitude or thwart her mother's matchmaking plans and insist on staying here with the children?

Her instincts urged her to avoid seeing him again just now. With these heavy emotions churning inside her, she was afraid seeing him now would be too dangerous. Her defenses were probably at the lowest point they had been since coming home to Pine Gulch. If he kissed her again, she wasn't at all certain she would have the strength to resist him.

But that was cowardly. She needed to see him again, if for no other reason than to express, now that she was more calm and rational than she had been on that river-bank, her deep and endless gratitude to him for giving her back these two dear children.

"I'll go, Mom."

"Are you sure? I don't mind."

"I need to do this. You're right. Will you watch the children for me?"

"I won't budge," her mother promised. "I'll sit right here and work on my crocheting the entire time. I promise."

"You don't have to literally watch them. You may certainly sit in the living room and check on them at various intervals."

"I'm not moving from this spot," Jan said. "Between Lou and me, we should be able to keep them safe."

The evening was lovely, unusually warm for mid-May. She drove through town with her window down, savoring the sights and sounds of Pine Gulch settling down for the night. Because it was Friday, the drive-in on the edge of the business district was crowded with cars. Teenagers hanging out, anxious for the end of the school year, young families grabbing a burger on payday, senior citizens treating their grandchildren to an ice-cream cone.

The flowers were beginning to bloom in some of the sidewalk planters along Main Street and everything was greening up beautifully. May was a beautiful time of year in eastern Idaho after the inevitable harshness of winter, brimming with life, rebirth, hope.

As she was right now.

She had heard about people suffering near-death encounters who claimed the experience gave them a new respect and appreciation for their life and the beauty of the world around them. That's how she felt right now. Even though it was her children who had nearly died, Laura knew she would have died right along with them if they hadn't been rescued.

She had Alex and Maya back now, along with a new appreciation for those flowers in carefully tended gardens, the mountains looming strong and steady over the town, the sense of home that permeated this place.

She drove toward those mountains now, to Cold Creek Canyon, where the creek flowed out of the high country and down through the valley. Her mother had given her directions to Taft's new house and she followed them, turning onto Cold Creek Road.

She found it no surprise that Jan knew Taft's address. Jan and her wide circle of friends somehow managed to keep their collective finger on the pulse of everything going on in town.

The area here along the creek was heavily wooded with Douglas fir and aspen trees and it took her a moment to find the mailbox with his house number. She peered through the trees but couldn't see anything of his house except a dark green metal roof that just about matched the trees in the fading light.

A bridge spanned the creek here and as she drove over it, she couldn't resist looking down at the silvery ribbon of water, darting over boulders and around fallen logs. Her children had been in that icy water, she thought, chilled all over again at how close she had come to losing everything.

She couldn't let it paralyze her. When the runoff eased a little, she needed to take Alex and Maya fishing in the river to help all of them overcome their fear of the water.

She stayed on the bridge for several moments, watching lightning-fast dippers crisscross the water for insects and a belted kingfisher perching on a branch without moving for long moments before he swooped into the water and nabbed a hapless hatchling trout.

As much as she enjoyed the serenity of the place, she finally gathered her strength and started her SUV again, following the winding driveway through the pines. She had to admit, she was curious to see his house. He had asked her to come see it, she suddenly remembered, and she had deflected the question and changed the subject, not wanting to intertwine their lives any further. She was sorry now that she hadn't come out while it was under construction.

The trees finally opened up into a small clearing and she caught her breath. His house was gorgeous: two stories of honey-colored pine logs and river rock with windows dominating the front and a porch that wrapped around the entire house so that he could enjoy the view of mountains and creek in every direction.

She loved it instantly, from the river-rock chimney rising out of the center to the single Adirondack chair on the porch, angled to look out at the mountains. She couldn't have explained it but she sensed warmth and welcome here.

Her heart pounded strangely in her ears as she

parked the SUV and climbed out. She saw a light inside the house but she also heard a rhythmic hammering coming from somewhere behind the structure.

That would be Taft. Somehow she knew it. She reached in for the pie her mother had made—why hadn't she thought of doing something like this for him?—and headed in the direction of the sound.

She found him in another clearing behind the house, framing up a building she assumed would be an outbuilding for the horses he had talked about. He had taken off his shirt to work the nail gun, and that leather tool belt he had used while he was working at the inn—not that she had noticed or anything—hung low over his hips. Muscles rippled in the gathering darkness and her stomach shivered.

Here was yet another image that could go in her own mental Taft Bowman beefcake calendar.

She huffed out a little breath, sternly reminding herself that standing and salivating over the man was *not* why she was here, and forced herself to move forward. Even though she wasn't trying to use stealth, he must not have heard her approach over the sound of the nail gun and the compressor used to power it, even when she was almost on top of him. He didn't turn around or respond in any way and she finally realized why when she saw white earbuds dangling down, tethered to a player in the back pocket of his jeans.

She had no idea what finally tipped him off to her presence, but the steady motion of the nail gun stopped, he paused for just a heartbeat and then he jerked his head around. In that instant, she saw myriad emotions cross his features—surprise, delight, resignation and something that looked very much like yearning before he shuttered his expression.

"Laura, hi."

"Hello."

"Just a second."

He pulled the earbuds out and tucked them away, then crossed to the compressor and turned off the low churning sound. The only sound to break the abrupt silence was the moaning of the wind in the treetops. Taft quickly grabbed a T-shirt slung over a nearby sawhorse and pulled it over his head, and she couldn't help the little pang of disappointment.

"I brought you a pie. My mother made it for you." She held out it, suddenly feeling slightly ridiculous at the meagerness of the offering.

"A pie?"

"I know, it's a small thing. Not at all commensurate with everything you did, but...well, it's something."

"Thank you. I love pie. And I haven't had anything to eat yet, so this should be great. I might just have pie for dinner."

He had a square bandage just under his hairline that made him look rather rakish, a startling white contrast to his dark hair and sun-warmed features.

"Your head. You were hurt during the rescue, weren't you?"

He shrugged. "No big deal. Just a little cut."

Out of nowhere, she felt the hot sting of tears threaten. "I'm sorry."

"Are you kidding? This is nothing. I would have gladly broken every limb, as long as it meant I could still get to the kids."

She stared at him there in the twilight, looking big and solid and dearly familiar, and a huge wave of love washed over her. This was Taft. Her best friend. The man she had loved forever, who could always make her laugh, who made her feel strong and powerful and able to accomplish anything she wanted.

Everything she had been trying to block out since she arrived back in Pine Gulch seemed to break through some invisible dam and she was filled, consumed, by her love for him.

Those tears burned harder and she knew she had to leave or she would completely embarrass herself by losing her slippery hold on control and sobbing all over him.

She drew in a shuddering breath. "I…I just wanted to say thank-you. Again, I mean. It's not enough. It will never be enough, but thank you. I owe you… everything."

"No, you don't. You owe me nothing. I was only doing my job."

"Only your job? Really?"

He gazed at her for a long moment and she prayed he couldn't see the emotions she could feel nearly choking her. "Okay, no," he finally said. "If I had been doing my job and following procedure, I would have waited for the swift-water tech team to come help me extricate them. I would have done everything by the book. I spend seventy percent of my time training my volunteers in the fire department *not* to do what I did today. This wasn't a job. It was much, much more."

A tear slipped free but she ignored it. She could barely make out his expression now in the twilight and had to hope the reverse was also true. She had to leave. Now, before she made a complete fool of herself.

"Well…I'm in your debt. You've got a room anytime you want at the inn."

"Thanks, I appreciate that."

She released a breath and nodded. "Well, thank you again. Enjoy the pie. I'll, uh, see you later."

She turned so swiftly that she nearly stumbled but caught herself and began to hurry back to her SUV while the tears she had struggled to contain broke free and trickled down her cheeks. She didn't know exactly why she was crying. Probably not a single reason. The stress of nearly losing her children, the joy of having them returned to her. And the sudden knowledge that she loved Taft Bowman far more than she ever had as a silly twenty-one-year-old girl.

"Laura, wait."

She shook her head, unable to turn around and reveal so much of her heart to him. As she should have expected, she only made it a few more steps before he caught up with her and turned her to face him.

He gazed down at her and she knew she must look horrible, blotchy-faced and red, with tears dripping everywhere.

"Laura," he murmured. Just that. And then with a groan he folded her into his arms, wrapping her in his heat and his strength. She shuddered again and could no longer stop the deluge. He held her as she sobbed out everything that suddenly seemed too huge and heavy for her to contain.

"I could have lost them."

"I know. I know." His arms tightened and his cheek

rested on her hair, and she realized this was exactly where she belonged. Nothing else mattered. She loved Taft Bowman, had always loved him, and more than that, she trusted him.

He was her hero in every possible way.

"And you." She sniffled. "You risked your life to go after them. You could have been carried away just as easily."

"I wasn't, though. All three of us made it through."

She tightened her arms around him and they stood that way for a long time with the creek rumbling over rocks nearby while the wind sighed in the trees and an owl hooted softly somewhere close and the crickets chirped for their mates.

Something changed between them in those moments. It reminded her very much of the first time he had kissed her, on that boulder overlooking River Bow Ranch, when she somehow knew that the world had shifted in some fundamental way and nothing would ever be the same.

After several moments, he moved his hands from around her and framed her face, his eyes reflecting the stars, then he kissed her with a tenderness that made her want to weep all over again.

It was a perfect moment, standing here with him as night descended, and she never wanted it to end. She wanted to savor everything—the soft cotton of his shirt, the leashed muscles beneath, his mouth, so firm and determined on hers.

She spread her palms on his back, pressing him closer, and he made a low sound in his throat, tightening his arms around her and deepening the kiss. She opened her mouth for him and slid her tongue out to dance with his while she pressed against those solid muscles, needing more.

His hand slipped beneath her shirt to the bare skin at her waist and she remembered just how he had always known how to touch her and taste her until she was crazy with need. She shivered, just a slight motion, but it was enough that he pulled his mouth away from hers, his breathing ragged and his eyes dazed.

He gazed down at her and she watched awareness return to his features like storm clouds crossing the moon, then he slid his hands away and took a step back.

"You asked me not to kiss you again. I'm sorry, Laura. I tried. I swear I tried."

She blinked, trying to force her brain to work. After a moment, she remembered the last time he had kissed her, in the room she had just finished decorating. She remembered her confusion and fear, remembered being so certain he would hurt her all over again if she let him.

That all seemed another lifetime ago. Had she really let her fears rule her common sense?

This was Taft, the man she had loved since she was twelve years old. He loved her and he loved her children. When she had climbed out of his brother's police vehicle and seen him there by the stretcher with his arms around Alex—and more, when she had seen that rope still tied to the tree and the churning, dangerous waters he had risked to save both of her children—she had known he was a man she could count on. He had been willing to break any rule, to give up everything to save her children.

I would have gladly broken every limb, as long as it meant I could still get to the kids.

He had risked his life. How much was she willing to risk?

Everything.

She gave him a solemn look, her heart jumping inside her chest, feeling very much as if *she* was the one about to leap into Cold Creek. "Technically, *I* could still kiss you, though, right?"

He stared at her and she saw his eyes darken with confusion and a wary sort of hope. That little glimmer was all she needed to step forward into the space between them and grab his strong, wonderful hands. She tugged him toward her and stood on tiptoe and pressed her mouth to the corner of his mouth.

He didn't seem to know how to respond for a moment and then he angled his mouth and she kissed him fully, with all the joy and love in her heart.

Much to her shock, he eased away again, his expression raw and almost despairing. "I can't do this back-and-forth thing, Laura. You have to decide. I love you. I never stopped, all this time. I think some part of me has just been biding my time, waiting for you to come home."

He pulled his hands away. "I know I hurt you ten years ago. I can't change that. If I could figure out how, I would in a heartbeat."

At that, she had to shake her head. "I wouldn't change anything," she said. "If things had been different, I wouldn't have Alex and Maya."

He released a breath. "I can tell you, I realized right after you left what a fool I had been, too stubborn and proud to admit I was hurting and not dealing with it well. And then I compounded my stupidity by not coming after you like I wanted to."

"I waited for you. I didn't date anyone for two years, even though I heard all the stories about...well, the Bandito and everything. If you had called or emailed or anything, I would have come home in an instant."

"I'm a different man than I was then. I want to think I've become a *better* man, but I've still probably picked up a few more nicks and bruises than I had then."

"Haven't we all?" she murmured.

"I need to tell you, I want everything, Laura. I want a home, family. I want those things with you, the same things I wanted a decade ago."

Joy burst through her. When he reached for her hand, she curled her fingers inside his, wondering how it was possible to go from the depths of hell to this brilliant happiness in the course of one day.

"I hope you know I love your children, too. Alex is such a great kid. I can think of a hundred things I would love to show him. How to ride a two-wheeler, how to throw a spitball, how to saddle his own horse. I think I could be a good father to him."

He brought their intertwined fingers to his heart. "And Maya. She's a priceless gift, Laura. I don't know exactly what she's going to need out of life, but I can promise you, right now, that I would spend the rest of my life doing whatever it takes to give it to her. I swear to you, I would watch over her, keep her safe, give her every chance she has to stretch her wings as

far as she can. I want to give her a place she can grow.
A place where she knows, every single minute, that
she's loved."

If she hadn't already been crazy in love with this
man, his words alone and his love for her fragile, vulnerable daughter would have done the trick. She gazed
up at him and felt tears of joy trickle out.

"I didn't mean to make you cry," he murmured, his
own eyes wet. The significance of that did not escape
her. The old Taft never would have allowed that sign
of emotion.

"I love you, Taft. I love you so very much."

Words seemed wholly inadequate, like offering a
caramel-apple pie in exchange for saving two precious
lives, so she did the only thing she could. She kissed
him again, holding him tightly to her. Could he feel the
joy pulsing through her, powerful, strong, delicious?

After long, wonderful moments, he eased away
again and she saw that he had been as moved as she
by the embrace.

"Will you come see the house now?" he asked.

Was this his subtle way of taking her inside to make
love? She wasn't quite sure she was ready to add one
more earthshaking experience on this most tumultu-
ous of days, but she did want to see his house. Besides
that, she trusted him completely. If she asked him to
wait, he would do it without question.

"Yes," she answered. He grinned and grabbed
her hand and together they walked through the trees
toward his house. He guided her up the stairs at the
side of the house that led first to the wide uncovered

porch and then inside to the great room with the huge windows.

She saw some similarities to the River Bow ranch house in the size of the two-story great room and the wall of windows, but there were differences, too. A balcony ringed the great room and she could see rooms leading off it.

How many bedrooms were in this place? she wondered. And why would a bachelor build this house that seemed made for a family?

The layout seemed oddly familiar to her and some of the details, as well. The smooth river-rock fireplace, the open floor plan, the random use of knobby, bulging, uniquely shaped logs as accents.

Only after he took her into the kitchen and she looked around at the gleaming appliances did all the details come together in her head.

"This is my house," she exclaimed.

"Our house," he corrected. "Remember how you used to buy log-home books and magazines and pore over them? I started building this house six months ago. It wasn't until you came back to Pine Gulch that I realized how I must have absorbed all those dreams inside me. I guess when I was planning the house, some of them must have soaked through my subconscious and onto the blueprints. I didn't even think about it until I saw you again."

It was a house that seemed built for love, for laughter, for children to climb over the furniture and dangle toys off the balcony.

"Do you like it?" he asked, and she saw that wariness in his eyes again that never failed to charm her far more than a teasing grin and lighthearted comment.

"I love everything about it, Taft. It's perfect. Beyond perfect."

He pulled her close again and as he held her there in the house he had built, she realized that love wasn't always a linear journey. Sometimes it took unexpected dips and curves and occasional sheer dropoffs. Yet somehow, despite the pain of their past, she and Taft had found their way together again.

This time, she knew, they were here to stay.

dou
their lo

Epilogue

His bride was late.

Taft stood in the entryway of the little Pine Gulch chapel under one of the many archways decorated with ribbons and flowers of red and bronze and deep green, greeting a few latecomers and trying his best not to fidget. He glanced at his watch. Ten minutes and counting when he was supposed to be tying the knot, and so far Laura was a no-show.

"She'll go through with it this time. The woman is crazy about you. Relax."

He glanced over at Trace, dressed in his best-man's Western-cut tuxedo. His brother looked disgustingly calm and Taft wanted to punch him.

"I know," he answered. For all his nerves, he didn't ⌐ that for a moment. Over the past six months, ⌐e had only deepened, become more rich and beautiful like the autumn colors around them. He had no worries about her pulling out of the wedding at the last minute.

He glanced through the doors of the chapel as if he could make her appear there. "I'm just hoping she's not having trouble somewhere. You don't have your radio on you, do you?"

Trace raised an eyebrow. "Uh, no. It's a wedding, in case you forgot. I don't need to have my radio squawking in the middle of the ceremony. I figured I could do without it for a few hours."

"Probably a good idea. You don't think she's been in an accident or something?"

Trace gave him a compassionate look. One of the hazards of working in public safety was this constant awareness of all the things that could go wrong in a person's life, but usually didn't. He was sure Trace worried about Becca and Gabi just as much as he fretted for Laura and the children.

"No. I'm sure there's a reasonable explanation. Why don't we check in with Caidy?"

That would probably be the logical course of action before he went off in a panic, since as maid of honor, she should be with Laura. "Yeah. Right. Good idea. Give me your phone."

"I can do it. That's what a best man is for, right?"

"Just give me your phone. Please?" he added, when Trace looked reluctant.

Trace reached into the inside pocket of his black suit jacket for his phone. "Hold on. I'll have to turn it back on. Wouldn't want any phones going off as you're taking your vows, either."

He waited impatiently, and after an eternity, his brother handed the activated phone over. Before he could find Caidy's number in the address book, the phone buzzed.

"Where are you?" he answered when he saw her name on the display.

"Taft? Why do you have Trace's phone?"

"I was just about to call you. What's wrong? Is Laura okay?"

"We're just pulling up to the church. I was calling to give you the heads-up that we might need a few more minutes. Maya woke up with a stomachache, apparently. She threw up before we left the cottage and then again on our way, all over her dress. We had to run back to the inn to find something else for her to wear."

"Is she all right now?"

"Eh. Okay, but not great. She's still pretty fretful. Laura's trying to soothe her. Have the organist keep playing, and as soon as we get there, we'll try to fix Maya up and calm her down a little more, then we can get this show on the road. Here we are now."

He saw the limo he had hired from Jackson Hole pulling up to the side door of the church, near the room set aside for the bridal party. "I see you. Thanks for calling."

He hung up the phone and handed it back to Trace. Ridge had joined them, he saw, and wore a little furrow of concern between his eyes.

"The girls okay?" Ridge asked.

"Maya's got a stomachache. Can you stall for a few more minutes?"

"Sure. How about a roping demonstration or something? I think I've got a lasso in the pickup."

He had to look closely at his older brother to see that Ridge was teasing, probably trying to ease the tension. Yeah, it wasn't really working. "I think a few more songs should be sufficient. I'm going to go check on Maya."

"What about the whole superstition about not seeing the bride before the wedding?" Trace asked. "As I recall, you and Ridge practically hog-tied me to keep me away from Becca before ours."

"These are special circumstances. You want to try to stop me, you're more than welcome. Good luck with that."

Neither brother seemed inclined to interfere, so Taft made his way through the church to the bridal-party room. Outside the door, he could hear the low hush of women's voices and then a little whimper. That tiny sound took away any remaining hesitation and he pushed open the door.

His gaze instinctively went to Laura. She was stunning in a cream-colored mid length lace confection, her silky golden hair pulled up in an intricate style that made her look elegant and vulnerable at the same time. Maya huddled in her lap, wearing only a white slip. Caidy and Jan stood by, looking helpless.

When Maya spotted him, she sniffed loudly. "Chief," she whimpered.

He headed over to the two females he loved with everything inside him and picked her up, heedless of his rented tux.

"What's the matter, little bug?"

"Tummy hurts."

She didn't seem to have a fever, from what he could tell.

"Do you think it's the giardiasis?" Jan asked.

He thought of the girl's abdominal troubles after her near-drowning, the parasite she had picked up from swallowing half the Cold Creek. "I wouldn't think so. She's been healthy for three months. Doc Dalton said she didn't need any more medicine."

His knees still felt weak whenever he thought of the miraculous rescue of the children. He knew he had been guided to them somehow. He found it equally miraculous that Alex had emerged unscathed from the ordeal and Maya's only lingering effect was the giardia bug she'd picked up.

She sure didn't look very happy right now, though. He wondered if he ought to call in Jake Dalton from the congregation to check on her, when he suddenly remembered a little tidbit of information that had slipped his mind in the joy-filled chaos leading up to the wedding.

"Maya, how many pieces of cake did you have last night at the rehearsal dinner?"

Two separate times he'd seen her with a plate of dessert but hadn't thought much about it until right now.

She shrugged, though he thought she looked a little guilty as she held up two fingers.

"Are you sure?"

She looked at her mother, then back at him, then used her other hand to lift up two more fingers.

Laura groaned. "No wonder she's sick this morning. I should have thought of that. We were all so distracted, I guess we must not have realized she made so many trips to the dessert table."

"I like cake," Maya announced.

He had to smile. "I do too, bug, but you should probably go easy on the wedding cake at the reception later."

"Okay."

He hugged her. "Feel better now?"

She nodded and wiped a fist at a few stray tears on her cheeks. She was completely adorable, and he still couldn't believe he had been handed this other miraculous gift, the chance to step in and be the father figure to this precious child and her equally precious brother.

"My dress is icky."

"You won't be able to wear your flower-girl dress with the fluffy skirt," Jan agreed. "We're going to have to wash it. It will probably be dry by the reception tonight, though. And look! I bought this red one for you for Christmas. We'll use that one at the wedding now and you'll look beautiful."

"You're a genius, Mom," Laura murmured.

"I have my moments," Jan said. She took her granddaughter from his arms to help her into the dress and fix her hair again.

"Crisis averted?" he asked Laura while Jan and Caidy fussed around Maya.

"I think so." She gave him a grateful smile and his heart wanted to burst with love for her, especially when she stepped closer to him and slipped her arms around his waist. "Are you sure you're ready to take on all this fun and excitement?"

He wrapped his arms around her, thinking how perfectly she fit there, how she filled up all the empty places that had been waiting all these years just for her. He kissed her forehead, careful not to mess up her pretty curls. "I've never been more sure of anything. I hope you know that."

"I do," she murmured.

He desperately wanted to kiss her, but had a feeling his sister and her mother wouldn't appreciate it in the middle of their crisis.

The door behind them opened and Alex burst through, simmering with the energy field that always seemed to surround him except when he was sleeping. "When is the wedding going to start? I'm tired of waiting."

"I know what you mean, kid," Taft said with a grin, stepping away from Laura a little so he could pull Alex over for a quick hug.

His family. He had waited more than ten years for this, and he didn't know if he had the patience to stand another minute's delay before all his half-buried dreams became reality.

"Okay. I think we're good here," Caidy said, as Jan adjusted the ribbon in the girl's brown hair.

"Doesn't she look great?"

"Stunning," he claimed.

Maya beamed at him and slipped her hand in his. "Marry now."

"That's a great idea, sweetheart." He turned to Laura. "Are you ready?"

She smiled at him, and as he gazed at this woman he had known for half his life and loved for most of that time, he saw the rest of their lives ahead of them, bright and beautiful, and filled with joy and laughter and love.

"I finally am," she said, reaching for his hand, and together they walked toward their future.

* * * * *

Dear Reader,

I am a big believer in celebrating milestones, and for Special Edition, this is a big one! Thirty years… it hardly seems possible, and yet April 1982 was indeed, yep, thirty years ago! When I walked into the Harlequin offices (only *twenty* years ago, but still), the first books I worked on were Special Edition. I loved the line instantly—for its breadth and its depth, and for its fabulous array of authors, some of whom I've been privileged to work with for twenty years, and some of whom are newer, but no less treasured, friends.

When it came time to plan our thirtieth anniversary celebration, we wanted to give our readers something from the heart—not to mention something from our very beloved April 2012 lineup. So many thanks to RaeAnne Thayne, Christine Rimmer, Susan Crosby, Christyne Butler, Gina Wilkins and Cindy Kirk for their contributions to *The Anniversary Party*. The Morgans, Diana and Frank, are celebrating their thirtieth anniversary along with us. Like us, they've had a great thirty years, and they're looking forward to many more. Like us, though there may be some obstacles along the way, they're getting their happily ever after.

Which is what we wish you, Dear Reader. Thanks for coming along for the first thirty years of Special Edition—we hope you'll be with us for many more!

We hope you enjoy *The Anniversary Party*.

Here's to the next thirty!

All the best,

Gail Chasan
Senior Editor, Special Edition

Chapter One
by RaeAnne Thayne

With the basket of crusty bread sticks she had baked that afternoon in one arm and a mixed salad—*insalata mista,* as the Italians would say—in the other, Melissa Morgan walked into her sister's house and her jaw dropped.

"Oh, my word, Ab! This looks incredible! When did you start decorating? A month ago?"

Predictably, Abby looked a little wild-eyed. Her sister was one of those type A personalities who always sought perfection, whether that was excelling in her college studies, where she'd emerged with a summa cum laude, or decorating for their parents' surprise thirtieth anniversary celebration.

Abby didn't answer for a moment. She was busy arranging a plant in the basket of a rusty bicycle resting against one wall so the greenery spilled over the top, almost to the front tire. Melissa had no idea how she'd managed it but somehow Abby had hung wooden lattice from her ceiling to form a faux pergola over her dining table. Grapevines, fairy lights and more greenery had been woven through the lattice and, at various intervals, candles hung in colored jars like something out of a Tuscan vineyard.

Adorning the walls were framed posters of Venice and the beautiful and calming Lake Como.

"It feels like a month," Abby finally answered, "but actually, I only started last week. Greg helped me hang the lattice. I couldn't have done it without him."

The affection in her sister's voice caused a funny little twinge inside Melissa. Abby and her husband had one of those perfect relationships. They clearly adored each other, no matter what.

She wished she could say the same thing about Josh. After a year of dating, shouldn't she have a little more confidence in their relationship? If someone had asked her a month ago if she thought her boyfriend loved her, she would have been able to answer with complete assurance in the affirmative, but for the past few weeks something had changed. He'd been acting so oddly—dodging phone calls, canceling plans, avoiding her questions.

He seemed to be slipping away more every day. As melodramatic as it sounded, she didn't know how she would survive if he decided to break things off.

Breathe, she reminded herself. She didn't want to ruin the anniversary dinner by worrying about Josh. For now, she really needed to focus on her wonderful parents and how very much they deserved this celebration she and Abby had been planning for a long time.

"You and Greg have really outdone yourself. I love all the little details. The old wine bottles, the flowers. Just beautiful. I know Mom and Dad will be thrilled with your hard work." She paused. "I can only see one little problem."

Abby looked vaguely panicked. "What? What's missing?"

Melissa shook her head ruefully. "Nothing. That's the problem. I was supposed to be helping you. That's why I'm here early, right? Have you left anything for me to do?"

"Are you kidding? I've still got a million things to do. The chicken cacciatore is just about ready to go into the oven. Why don't you help me set the table?"

"Sure," she said, following her sister into the kitchen.

"You talked to Louise, right?" Abby asked.

"Yes. She had everything ready when I stopped at her office on my way over here. I've got a huge gift basket in the car. You should see it. She really went all out. Biscotti, gourmet cappuccino mix, even a bottle of prosecco."

"What about the tickets and the itinerary?" Abby had that panicked look again.

"Relax, Abs. It's all there. She's been amazing. I think she just might be as scarily organized as you are."

Abby made a face. "Did you have a chance to go over the details?"

"She printed everything out and included a copy for us, as well as Mom and Dad. In addition to the plane tickets and the hotel information and the other goodies, she sent over pamphlets, maps, even an Italian-English dictionary and a couple of guidebooks."

"Perfect! They're going to be so surprised."

"Surprised and happy, I hope," Melissa answered, loading her arms with the deep red chargers and honey-gold plates her sister indicated, which perfectly matched the theme for the evening.

"How could they be anything else? They finally have the chance to enjoy the perfect honeymoon they missed out on the first time." Abby smiled, looking more than a little starry-eyed. Despite being married for several years, her sister was a true romantic.

"This has to be better than the original," she said. "The bar was set pretty low thirty years ago, judging by all the stories they've told us over the years. Missed trains, lousy hotels, disappearing luggage."

"Don't forget the pickpocket that stole their cash and passports."

Melissa had to smile. Though their parents' stories always made their honeymoon thirty years ago sound dismal, Frank and Diane always laughed when they shared them, as if they had viewed the whole thing as a huge adventure.

She wanted that. She wanted to share that kind of joy and laughter and tears with Josh. The adventure that was life.

Her smile faded, replaced by that ache of sadness that always seemed so close these days. *Oh, Josh.* She reached into the silverware drawer, avoiding her sister's gaze.

"Okay. What's wrong?" Abby asked anyway.

She forced a smile. "Nothing. I'm just a little tired, that's all."

"Late night with Josh?" her sister teased.

Before she could stop them, tears welled up and spilled over. She blinked them back but not before her sharp-eyed sister caught them.

"What did I say?" Abby asked with a stunned look.

"Nothing. I just...I didn't have a late night with Josh. Not last night, not last week, not for the last two weeks. He's avoiding my calls and canceled our last two dates. Even when we're together, it's like he's not there. I know he's busy at work but...I think he's planning to break up with me."

Abby's jaw sagged and Melissa saw shock and something else, something furtive, shift across Abby's expression.

"That can't be true. It just...can't be."

She wanted to believe that, too. "I'm sorry. I shouldn't have said anything. Forget it. You've worked so hard to make this night perfect and I don't want to ruin it."

Abby shook her head. "You need to put that wacky idea out of your head right now. Josh is crazy about you. It's clear to anybody who has ever seen the two of you together for five seconds. He couldn't possibly be thinking of breaking things off."

"I'm sure you're right," she lied. Too much evidence pointed otherwise. Worst of all was the casual kiss good-night the past few times she'd seen him, instead of one of their deep, emotional, soul-sharing kisses that made her toes curl.

"I'm serious, Missy. Trust me on this. I'm absolutely positive he's not planning to break up with you. Not Josh. He loves you. In fact…"

She stopped, biting her lip, and furiously turned back to the chicken.

"In fact what?"

Abby's features were evasive. "In fact, would he be out right now with Greg buying the wine and champagne for tonight if he didn't want to have anything to do with the Morgan family?"

Out of the corner of her gaze, Melissa saw that amazingly decorated dining room again, the magical setting her sister had worked so hard to create for their parents who loved each other dearly. She refused to ruin this night for Abby and the rest of her family. For now, she would focus on the celebration and forget the tiny cracks in her heart.

She pasted on a smile and grabbed the napkins, with their rings formed out of entwined grapevine hearts. "You're right. I'm being silly. I'm sure everything will be just fine. Anyway, tonight is for Mom and Dad. That's the important thing."

Abby gave her a searching look and Melissa couldn't help thinking that even with the worry lines on her forehead, Abby seemed to glow tonight.

"It is about them, isn't it?" Abby murmured. Though Melissa's arms were full, her sister reached around the plates and cutlery to give her a hug. "Trust me, baby sister. Everything will be just fine."

Melissa dearly wanted to believe her and as she

returned to the dining room, she did her very best to ignore the ache of fear that something infinitely dear was slipping away.

"Hello? Are you still in there?"

His friend Greg's words jerked Josh out of his daze and he glanced up. "Yeah. Sorry. Did you say something?"

"Only about three times. I've been asking your opinion about the champagne and all I'm getting in return is a blank stare. You're a million miles away, man, which is not really helping out much here."

This just might be the most important day of his life. Who could blame a guy if he couldn't seem to string two thoughts together?

"Sorry. I've got a lot of things on my mind."

"And champagne is obviously not one of those things."

He made a face. "It rarely is. I'm afraid I'm more of a Sam Adams kind of guy."

"I hear you. Why do you think I asked you to come along and help me pick out the wine and champagne for tonight?"

He had wondered that himself. "Because my car has a bigger trunk?"

Greg laughed, which eased Josh's nerves a little. He had to admit, he had liked the guy since he met him a year ago when he first started dating Melissa. Josh was married to Melissa's sister, Abby, and if things worked out the way he hoped, they would be brothers-in-law in the not-so-distant future.

"It's only the six of us for dinner," Greg reminded

him. "I'm not exactly buying cases here. So what do you think?"

He turned back to the racks of bottles. "No idea. Which one is more expensive?"

Greg picked one up with a fancy label that certainly looked pricey.

"Excellent choice." The snooty clerk who had mostly been ignoring them since they walked in finally deigned to approach them.

"You think so?" Greg asked. "We're celebrating a big occasion."

"You won't be disappointed, I assure you. What else can I help you find?"

Sometime later—and with considerably lightened wallets—the two of them carried two magnums of champagne and two bottles of wine out to Josh's car.

"I, uh, need to make one last quick stop," he said after pulling into traffic. "Do you mind waiting?"

"No problem. The party doesn't start for another two hours. We've got plenty of time."

When Josh pulled up in front of an assuming storefront a few moments later, Greg looked at the sign above the door then back at him with eyebrows raised. "Wow. Seriously? Tonight? I thought Abby was jumping the gun when she said she suspected you were close to proposing. She's always right, that beautiful wife of mine. Don't tell her I said that."

Josh shifted, uncomfortably aware his fingers were shaking a little as he undid his seatbelt. "I bought the ring two weeks ago. When the jeweler told me it would be ready today, I figured that was a sign."

"You're a brave man to pick a ring out without her."

Panic clutched at his gut again, but he took a deep breath and pushed it away. He wanted to make his proposal perfect. Part of that, to his mind, was the element of surprise.

"I found a bridal magazine at Melissa's apartment kind of hidden under a stack of books and she had the page folded down on this ring. I snapped a quick picture with my phone and took that in to the jeweler."

"Nice." Greg's admiring look settled his stomach a little.

"I figure, if she doesn't like it, we can always reset the stone, right?"

"So when are you going to pop the question?"

"I haven't figured that out yet. I thought maybe when I take her home after the party tonight, we might drive up to that overlook above town."

"That could work."

"What about you? How did you propose to Abby?"

"Nothing very original, I'm afraid. I took her to dinner at La Maison Marie. She loves that place. Personally, I think you're only paying for overpriced sauce, but what can you do? Anyway, after dinner, she kept acting like she was expecting something. I *did* take her along to shop for rings a few weeks earlier but hadn't said anything to her since. She seemed kind of disappointed when the dessert came and no big proposal. So we were walking around on the grounds after dinner and we walked past this waterfall and pond she liked. I pretended I tripped over something and did a stupid little magician sleight of hand and pulled out the ring box."

"Did you do the whole drop-to-your-knee thing?"

"Yeah. It seemed important to Abby. Women remember that kind of thing."

"I hope I don't forget that part."

"Don't sweat it. When the moment comes, whatever you do will be right for the two of you, I promise."

"I hope so."

The depth of his love for Melissa still took him by surprise. He loved her with everything inside him and wanted to give her all the hearts and flowers and romance she could ever want.

"It will be," Greg said. "Anyway, look at how lousy Frank and Diane's marriage started out. Their honeymoon sounded like a nightmare but thirty years later they can still laugh about it."

That was what he wanted with Melissa. Thirty years—and more—of laughter and joy and love.

He just had to get through the proposal first.

Chapter Two
by Christine Rimmer

"Frank. The light is yellow. Frank!" Diana Morgan stomped the passenger-side floor of the Buick. Hard. If only she had the brakes on her side.

Frank Morgan pulled to a smooth stop as the light went red. "There," he said, in that calm, deep, untroubled voice she'd always loved. "We're stopped. No need to wear a hole in the floor."

Diana glanced over at her husband of thirty years. She loved him so much. There were a whole lot of things to worry about in life, but Frank's love was the one thing Diana never doubted. He belonged to her, absolutely, as she belonged to him, and he'd given her two beautiful, perfect daughters. Abby and Melissa were all grown up now.

The years went by way too fast.

Diana sent her husband another glance. Thirty years together. Amazing. She still loved just looking at him. He was the handsomest man she'd ever met, even at fifty-seven. Nature had been kind to him. He had all his hair and it was only lightly speckled with gray. She smoothed her own shoulder-length bob. No gray there, either. Her hair was still the same auburn shade it had been when she married him. Only in her case, nature didn't have a thing to do with it.

A man only grew more distinguished over the years. A woman had to work at it.

The light turned green. Frank hit the gas.

Too hard, Diana thought. But she didn't say a word. She only straightened her teal-blue silk blouse, re-crossed her legs and tried not to make impatient, worried noises. Frank was a wonderful man. But he drove too fast.

Abby and her husband, Greg, were having them over for dinner tonight. They were on their way there now—to Abby's house. Diana was looking forward to the evening. But she was also dreading it. Something was going on with Abby. A mother knows these things.

And something was bothering Melissa, too. Diana's younger daughter was still single. She'd been going out with Josh Wright for a year now. It was a serious relationship.

But was there something wrong between Josh and Melissa? Diana had a sense about these things, a sort of radar for emotional disturbances, especially when it came to her daughters. Right now, tonight, Diana had a suspicion that something wasn't right—both between Melissa and Josh *and* between Abby and Greg.

"Remember Venice?" Frank gave her a fond glance.

She smiled at him—and then stiffened. "Frank. Eyes on the road."

"All right, all right." He patiently faced front again. "Remember that wonderful old hotel on the Grand Canal?"

She made a humphing sound. "It was like the rest of our honeymoon. Nothing went right."

"I loved every moment of it," he said softly.

She reminded him, "You know what happened at that hotel in Venice, how they managed to lose our luggage somewhere between the front desk and our room. How hard can it be, to get the suitcases to the right room? And it smelled a bit moldy in the bathroom, didn't you think?"

"All I remember is you, Diana. Naked in the morning light." He said it softly. Intimately.

She shivered a little, drew in a shaky breath and confessed, "Oh, yes. That. I remember that, too." It was one of the best things about a good marriage. The shared memories. Frank had seen her naked in Venice when they were both young. Together, they had heard Abby's first laugh, watched Melissa as she learned to walk, staggering and falling, but then gamely picking herself right back up and trying again. Together, they had made it through all those years that drew them closer, through the rough times as well as the happy ones....

A good marriage.

Until very recently, she'd been so sure that Abby and Greg were happy. But were they? Really? And what about Melissa and Josh?

Oh, Lord. Being a mother was the hardest job in the world. They grew up. But they stayed in your heart. And when they were suffering, you ached right along with them.

"All right," Frank said suddenly in an exasperated tone. "You'd better just tell me, Diana. You'd better just say it, whatever it is."

Diana sighed. Deeply. "Oh, Frank…"

"Come on," he coaxed, pulling to another stop at yet another stoplight—at the very last possible second. She didn't even stomp the floor that time, she was that upset. "Tell me," he insisted.

Tears pooled in her eyes and clogged her throat. She sniffed them back. "I wasn't going to do it. I wasn't going to interfere. I wasn't even going to say a word…"

He flipped open the armrest and whipped out a tissue. "Dry your eyes."

"Oh, Frank…" She took the tissue and dabbed at her lower lid. If she wasn't careful, her makeup would be a total mess.

"Now," Frank said, reaching across to pat her knee. "Tell me about it. Whatever it is, you know you'll feel better once we've talked it over."

The light changed. "Go," she said on a sob.

He drove on. "I'm waiting."

She sniffed again. "I think something's wrong between Abby and Greg. And not only that, there's something going on with Melissa, too. I think Melissa's got…a secret, you know? A secret that is worrying her terribly."

"Why do you think something's going on between Abby and Greg?"

"I sensed it. You know how sensitive I am— Oh,

God. Do you think Abby and Greg are breaking up? Do you think he might be seeing someone else?"

"Whoa. Diana. Slow down."

"Well, I am *worried.* I am *so* worried. And Melissa. She is suffering. I can hear it in her voice when I talk to her."

"But you haven't told me *why* you think there might be something wrong—with Melissa, or between Abby and Greg. Did Abby say something to you?"

"Of course not. She wants to protect me."

"What about Melissa?"

"What do you *mean,* what about Melissa?"

"Well, did you *ask* her if something is bothering her?"

Another sob caught in Diana's throat. She swallowed it. "I couldn't. I didn't want to butt in."

Frank eased the car to the shoulder and stopped. "Diana," he said. That was all. Just her name.

It was more than enough. "Don't you look at me like that, Frank Morgan."

"Diana, I hate to say this—"

"Then don't. Just don't. And why are we stopped? We'll be late. Even with family, you know I always like to be on time."

"Diana…"

She waved her soggy tissue at him. "Drive, Frank. Just drive."

He leaned closer across the console. "Sweetheart…"

She sagged in her seat. "Oh, fine. What?"

"You know what you're doing, don't you?" He said it gently. But still. She knew exactly what he was getting at and she didn't like it one bit.

She sighed and dropped the wadded tissue in the little wastepaper bag she always carried in the car. "Well, I know you're bound to tell me, now don't I?"

He took her hand, kissed the back of it.

"Don't try to butter me up," she muttered.

"You're jumping to conclusions again," he said tenderly.

"Am not."

"Yes, you are. You've got nothin'. Zip. Admit it. No solid reason why you think Melissa has a secret or why you think Abby and Greg are suddenly on the rocks."

"I don't need a solid reason. I can *feel* it." She laid her hand over her heart. "Here."

"You know it's very possible that what's really going on is a surprise anniversary party for us, don't you?"

Diana smoothed her hair. "What? You mean tonight?"

"That's right. Tonight."

"Oh, I suppose. It could be." She pictured their dear faces. She loved them so much. "They are the sweetest girls, aren't they?"

"The best. I'm the luckiest dad in the world—not to mention the happiest husband."

Diana leaned toward him and kissed him. "You *are* a very special man." She sank back against her seat— and remembered how worried she was. "But Frank, if this *is* a party, it's still not *it*."

"It?" He looked bewildered. Men could be so thickheaded sometimes.

Patiently, she reminded him, "The awful, secret things that are going on with our daughters."

He bent in close, kissed her cheek and then brushed his lips across her own. "We are going to dinner at our daughter's house," he whispered. "We are going to have a wonderful time. You are not going to snoop around trying to find out if something's wrong with Abby. You're not going to worry about Melissa."

"I hate you, Frank."

"No, you don't. You love me *almost* as much as I love you."

She wrinkled her nose at him. "More. I love you more."

He kissed her again. "Promise you won't snoop and you'll stop jumping to conclusions?"

"And if I don't, what? We'll sit here on the side of the road all night?"

"Promise."

"Fine. All right. I promise."

He touched her cheek, a lovely, cherishing touch. "Can we go to Abby's now?"

"I'm not the one who stopped the car."

He only looked at her reproachfully.

She couldn't hold out against him. She never could. "Oh, all right. I've promised, already, okay? Now, let's go."

With a wry smile, he retreated back behind the wheel and eased the car forward into the flow of traffic again.

Abby opened the door. "Surprise!" Abby, Greg, Melissa and Josh all shouted at once. They all started clapping.

Greg announced, "Happy Anniversary!" The rest of

them chimed in with "Congratulations!" and "Thirty years!" and "Wahoo!"

Frank was laughing. "Well, what do you know?"

Diana said nothing. One look in her older daughter's big brown eyes and she knew for certain that she wasn't just imagining things. Something was going on in Abby's life. Something important.

They all filed into the dining room, where the walls were decorated with posters of the Grand Canal and the Tuscan countryside, of the Coliseum and the small, beautiful town of Bellagio on Lake Como. The table was set with Abby's best china and tall candles gave a golden glow.

Greg said, "We thought, you know, an Italian theme—in honor of your honeymoon."

"It's lovely," said Diana, going through the motions, hugging first Greg and then Josh.

"Thank you," said Frank as he clapped his son-in-law on the back and shook hands with Josh.

Melissa came close. "Mom." She put on a smile. But her eyes were as shadowed as Abby's. "Happy thirtieth anniversary."

Diana grabbed her and hugged her. No doubt about it. Melissa looked miserable, too.

Yes, Diana had promised Frank that she would mind her own business.

But, well, sometimes a woman just couldn't keep that kind of promise. Sometimes a woman had to find a way to get to the bottom of a bad situation for the sake of the ones she loved most of all.

By the end of the evening, no matter what, Diana

would find out the secrets her daughters were keeping from her.

Frank leaned close. "Don't even think about it."

She gave him her sweetest smile. "Happy anniversary, darling."

Chapter Three
by Susan Crosby

Abby Morgan DeSena and her husband, Greg, had hosted quite a few dinner parties during their three years of marriage, but none as special as this one—a celebration of Abby's parents' thirtieth wedding anniversary. Abby and her younger sister, Melissa, had spent weeks planning the Italian-themed party as a sweet reminder for their parents of their honeymoon, and now that the main meal was over, Abby could say, well, so far, so good.

For someone who planned everything down to the last detail, that was high praise. They were on schedule. First, antipasti and wine in the living room, then chicken cacciatore, crusty bread sticks and green salad in the dining room.

But for all that the timetable had been met and the

food praised and devoured, an air of tension hovered over the six people at the table, especially between Melissa and her boyfriend, Josh, who were both acting out of character.

"We had chicken cacciatore our first night in Bellagio, remember, Diana?" Abby's father said to her mother as everyone sat back, sated. "And lemon sorbet in prosecco."

"The waiter knocked my glass into my lap," Diana reminded him.

"Your napkin caught most of it, and he fixed you another one. He even took it off the tab. On our newlywed budget, it made a difference." He brought his wife's hand to his lips, his eyes twinkling. "And it was delicious, wasn't it? Tart and sweet and bubbly."

Diana blushed, making Abby wonder if the memory involved more than food. It was inspiring seeing her parents so openly in love after thirty years.

Under the table, Abby felt her hand being squeezed and looked at her own beloved husband. Greg winked, as if reading her mind.

"Well, we don't have sorbet and prosecco," Abby said, standing and stacking dinner plates. "But we certainly have dessert. Please sit down, Mom. You're our guest. Melissa and I will take care of everything."

It didn't take long to clear the table.

"Mom and Dad loved the dinner, didn't they?" Melissa asked as they entered Abby's contemporary kitchen.

"They seemed to," Abby answered, although unsure whether she believed her own words. Had her parents noticed the same tension Abby had? Her mother's gaze had flitted from Melissa to Josh to Abby to Greg all evening, as if searching for clues. It'd made Abby more nervous with every passing minute, and on a night she'd been looking forward to, a night of sweet surprises.

"How about you? Did you enjoy the meal?" Abby asked Melissa, setting dishes in the sink, then started the coffeemaker brewing. "You hardly touched your food."

She shrugged. "I guess I snacked on too many bread sticks before dinner."

Abby took out a raspberry tiramisu from the refrigerator while studying her sister, noting how stiffly Melissa held herself, how shaky her hands were as she rinsed the dinner plates. She seemed fragile. It wasn't a word Abby usually applied to her sister. The conversation they'd had earlier in the evening obviously hadn't set Melissa's mind at ease, but Abby didn't know what else to say to her tightly wrung sister. Only time—and Josh—could relieve Melissa's anxiety.

Abby set the fancy dessert on the counter next to six etched-crystal parfait glasses.

Melissa approached, drying her hands, then picked up one of the glasses. "Grandma gave these to you, didn't she?"

"Mmm-hmm. Three years ago as a wedding present. I know it's a cliché, but it seems like yesterday." Abby smiled at her sister, remembering the wedding, revisiting her wonderful marriage. She couldn't ask for a better husband, friend and partner than Greg. "Grandma plans to give you the other six glasses at your wedding. When we both have big family dinners, we can share them. It'll be our tradition."

Melissa's face paled. Her eyes welled. Horrified, Abby dropped the spoon and reached for her.

"I—I'll grab the gift basket from your office," Melissa said, taking a couple steps back then rushing out.

Frustrated, Abby pressed her face into her hands. If she were the screaming type, she would've screamed. If she were a throw-the-pots-around type, she would've done that, too, as noisily as possible. It would've felt *good*.

"I thought Melissa was in here with you," said a male voice from behind her.

Abby spun around and glared at Josh Wright, the source of Melissa's problems—and subsequently Abby's—as he peeked into the kitchen. He could be the solution, too, if only he'd act instead of sitting on his hands.

"She's getting the anniversary gift from my office," Abby said through gritted teeth, digging deep for the composure she'd inherited from her father.

Josh came all the way into the room. He looked as strained as Melissa. "Need some help?" he asked, shoving his hands into his pockets instead of going in search of Melissa.

"Coward." Abby began dishing up six portions of tiramisu.

"Guilty," Josh said, coming up beside her. "Give me a job. I can't sit still."

"You can pour the decaf into that carafe next to the coffeemaker."

Full of nervous energy, his hands shaking as

much as Melissa's had earlier, he got right to the task, fumbling at every step, slopping coffee onto the counter.

"Relax, would you, Josh?" Abby said, exasperated. "You're making everyone jumpy, but especially Melissa. My sister is her mother's daughter, you know. They both have a flair for the dramatic, but this time Melissa is honestly thrown by your behavior. She's on the edge, and it's not of her own making."

"But it'll all come out okay in the end?"

The way he turned the sentence into a question had Abby staring at him. He and her kid sister were a study in contrasts, Melissa with her black hair and green eyes, Josh all blond and blue-eyed. They'd been dating for a year, were head over heels in love with each other, seeming to validate the theory that opposites attract. It was rare that they weren't touching or staring into each other's eyes, communicating silently.

Tonight was different, however, and Abby knew why. She just didn't know if they would all survive the suspense.

"Whether or not it all turns out okay in the end depends on how long you take to pop the question," Abby said, dropping her voice to a whisper.

"You know I'm planning the perfect proposal," he whispered back. "Your husband gave me advice, but if you'd like to add yours, I'm listening."

She couldn't tell him that Melissa thought he was about to break up with her—that was hers to say. But Abby could offer some perspective.

"Here's my advice, Josh, and it has nothing to do with how to set a romantic scene that she'll remember the rest of her life. My advice is simple—do it sooner rather than later." She spoke in a normal tone again, figuring even if someone came into the room, they wouldn't suspect what she and Josh were talking about. "When Greg and I were in college, I misunderstood something he said. Instead of asking him to clarify it, I stewed. And stewed some more. I blew it all out of proportion."

She dug deep into memories she'd long ago put aside. "Here's what happens to a couple at times like that. He asks what's wrong, and she says it's nothing. He asks again. She *insists* it's nothing. A gulf widens that can't be crossed because there's no longer a bridge between them, one you used to travel easily. It doesn't even matter how much love you share. Once trust is gone, once the ability to talk to each other openly and freely goes away, the relationship begins to unravel. Sometimes it takes weeks, sometimes months, even years, but it happens and there's no fixing it."

"But you fixed it."

They almost hadn't, Abby remembered. They came so close to breaking up. "At times like that, it can go either way. Even strong partners struggle sometimes in a marriage."

"How do you get through those times?"

"You put on a smile for everyone, then you try to work it out alone together so that no one else gets involved."

"Don't you talk to your mom? She's had a long, successful marriage. She'd give good advice, wouldn't she?"

Abby smiled as she pictured her sweet, sometimes overwrought mother. "Mom's the last one I'd ask for advice," she said.

"I'm going to see what's taking so long," Diana said to her husband, laying her napkin on the table.

"Diana." Implied in his tone of voice were the words he didn't speak aloud—*Don't borrow trouble.*

"I'm sure they'll be right out," Greg said, standing, suddenly looking frantic. Her cool, calm son-in-law never panicked.

It upped her determination to see what was wrong. Because something definitely was.

"I'm going." Diana headed toward the kitchen. She could hear Abby speaking quietly.

"I adore my mother, but she makes mountains out of molehills. Greg and I are a team. We keep our problems to ourselves. And you know she would take my side, as any parent would, and that isn't fair to Greg. She might hold on to her partiality long after I've forgotten the argument. So you see, Josh, sometimes the best way to handle personal problems is to keep other people in the dark. Got it?"

"Clear as a bell."

Diana slapped a hand over her mouth and slid a few feet along the wall outside the kitchen before she let out an audible gasp. Her first born *was* keeping her in the dark about something, just as Diana had suspected. And Frank had pooh-poohed the whole thing.

Men just didn't get it. It wasn't called women's intuition for nothing—and she wasn't just a woman but a mother. Mothers saw every emotion on their children's faces, knew every body movement.

She'd *known* something was wrong with Abby. Now it'd been verified, not by rumor but by the person in question, no less. Abby and Greg were on the verge of separating. Her daughter had hidden their problems, not seeking advice from the one who loved her most in the world. Diana could've helped, too, she was sure of it.

Keep other people in the dark. The words stung. She wasn't "other people." She was Abby's mother.

And what about Melissa? What was her problem— because she definitely had one, something big, too. Had she confided in Abby?

Diana moved out of range, not wanting to hear more distressing words, not on the anniversary of the most wonderful day of her life. But she had to tell Frank what she'd learned, had to share the awful news with her own partner so that she could make it through the rest of the evening.

At least she could count on Frank to understand.

She hoped.

Chapter Four
by Christyne Butler

Don't think, don't feel.

Just keep breathing and you'll get through this night unscathed.

Unscathed, but with a broken heart.

Melissa squared her shoulders, brushed the wetness from her cheeks and heaved a shuddering breath that shook her all the way to her toes.

There. Don't you feel calmer?

No, she didn't, but that wasn't anyone's fault but her own.

She'd fallen in love with Josh on their very first date and after tonight, she'd probably never see him again.

The past two weeks had been crazy at her job. Trying to make it through what had been ten hours without her usual caffeine fix, having decided that two cups of coffee and three diet sodas a day weren't the best thing for her, had taken its toll. She'd been moody and pissy and okay, she was big to admit it, a bit dramatic.

Hey, she was her mother's daughter.

But none of that explained why the man of her dreams was going to break her heart.

Another deep breath did little to help, but it would have to do. Between helping her sister plan tonight's party and Josh's strange behavior, Melissa knew she was holding herself together with the thinnest of threads.

The scent of fresh coffee drifted through the house and Melissa groaned. Oh, how she ached for a hot cup, swimming in cream and lots of sugar.

Pushing the thought from her head, she picked up the gift basket that held everything her parents would need for a perfect second honeymoon in Italy. There was a small alcove right next to the dining room, a perfect place to stash it until just the right moment.

Turning, she headed for the door of her sister's office when the matching antique photo frames on a nearby bookshelf caught her eye.

The one on the right, taken just a few short years ago, was of Abby and Greg standing at the altar just after being presented to their friends and family as Mr. and Mrs. Gregory DeSena. Despite the elaborate setting, and the huge bridal party standing on either side of them, Melissa right there next to her sister, Abby and Greg only had eyes for each other. In fact, the photographer had captured the picture just as Greg had gently wiped a tear from her sister's cheek.

The other photograph, a bit more formal in monochrome colors of black and white, showed her mother and father on their wedding day. Her mother looked so young, so beautiful, so thin. Daddy was as handsome as ever in his tuxedo, his arm around his bride, his hand easily spanning her waist. The bridal bouquet was larger and over-the-top, typical for the early 80's, but her mother's dress...

Melissa squeezed tighter to the basket, the cellophane crinkling loudly in the silent room.

Abby had planned her wedding with the precision of an army general, right down to her chiffon, A-line silhouette gown with just enough crystal bling along the shoulder straps to give a special sparkle. Their mother looked the opposite, but just as beautiful wearing her own mother's gown, a vintage 1960 beauty of satin, lace and tulle with a circular skirt that cried out for layers of crinoline, a square-neck bodice and sleeves that hugged her arms.

A dress that Melissa had always seen herself wearing one day.

The day she married Josh.

Of course, she'd change into something short and sexy and perfect for dancing the night away after the ceremony, but—

"Oh, what does it matter!" Melissa said aloud. "It's not going to happen! It's never going to happen! Josh doesn't want to date you anymore, much less even think about getting down on one knee."

She exited the room and hurried down the long hall, tucking the basket just out of sight. They would have dessert, present the gift and then she would find a way to get Josh to take her home as soon as possible.

For the last time.

This was all Greg's fault.

As heartbreaking as it was, because she and Frank had always loved Greg, Diana knew deep in her heart that the man they'd welcomed in their home, into their hearts, was on the verge of walking out on their daughter.

How could Greg do this to Abby?

They were perfect together, complemented each other so well because they were so alike. Levelheaded, organized to a fault, methodical even.

Diana paused and grabbed hold of the stairway landing.

Could that be it?

Could Abby and Greg be too much alike? Had her son-in-law found someone else? Someone cute and bubbly who hung on his every word like it was gold?

Abby had mentioned a coworker of Greg's they'd run into one night while out to dinner. She'd said he'd been reluctant to introduce them, which seemed strange as the woman had literally gushed at how much she enjoyed working with Abby's husband when she'd stopped by their table.

The need to get to Frank, to squeeze his hand and have him comfort her, rolled over Diana. She needed him to tell her that everything would be all right, that she'd been right all along, and promise her they'd fight tooth and nail for their daughter so she didn't lose this beautiful home.

"Mom?"

Diana looked up and found Melissa standing there.

"Are you okay?" Melissa asked. "You look a little pale."

"I'm fine."

"You've got a death grip on the railing."

Diana immediately released her hold. "I just got a bit light-headed for a moment."

Concern filled her daughter's beautiful eyes. She motioned to the steps that led to the second floor. "Here, let's sit."

"But your sister is—"

"Perfectly capable of pulling dessert together all on her own," Melissa took her arm and the two of them sat. "Disgustingly capable, as we both know."

Diana sat, basically because she had no choice, taking the time to really look at her daughter. She'd been crying. Her baby suffered the same fate as she did when tears came—puffy eyes. And while Melissa had been acting strange during dinner, this was the first true evidence Diana had that something was terribly wrong.

"Darling, you seem a bit…off this evening." Diana kept her tone light after a few minutes of silence passed. "How is everything with you? You didn't eat very much tonight."

Melissa stared at her clenched hands. "Everything is just fine, Mother. It's been a long week and I'm very tired."

"Yes, you said you've been working long hours. That's probably cut into your free time with Josh."

"Y-yes, it has, but I don't think that's going to be a problem much longer."

"What does that mean?"

Melissa rose, one hand pressed against her stomach. "It's nothing. You were right. We should get back into the dining room. You know how Abby gets when things go off schedule."

Yes, she did know. Oh, the divorce was going to upset Abby's tidy world, but that didn't mean that Diana wouldn't be there for her other daughter, as well. She still had no idea what was bothering her youngest, but she would find out before this evening was through.

And she would make things right.

For both her girls.

She'd easily found the time to attend Abby's debates, girl scout meetings and band concerts and never missed a dance recital, theatre production or football game while Melissa was on the cheerleading squad. Her daughters might be grown, but they still needed their mother.

Now more than ever.

Diana stood, as well. "Yes, let's go back and join everyone."

They walked into the room and Diana's gaze locked with Frank's. Her husband watched her every step as she moved around the table to retake her seat next to him. Thirty years of marriage honed his deduction skills to a razor-sharp point, and she knew that he knew she'd found out something.

"Okay, let's get this celebration going." Greg spoke from where he stood at the buffet filling tall fluted glasses with sparkling liquid, having already popped open the bottle. "Josh, why don't you hand out the champagne to everyone?"

Frank leaned in close. "What's wrong?"

Diana batted her eyes, determined not to cry as his gentle and caring tone was sure to bring on the waterworks. "Not now, darling."

"So you were worried for nothing?"

"Of course not. I was right all along—" She cut off her words when Abby came in with a tray of desserts in her hands. "Dear, can I help with those?"

"No, you stay seated, Mom. It'll only take me a moment to hand these out."

True to her words, the etched-crystal parfait dishes were soon at everyone's place setting and, immediately after, Josh placed a glass in front of Frank and Diana.

Diana watched as he then went back to get two more for Greg and Abby and one last trip for the final two glasses.

"Here you go, sweetheart." He moved in behind Melissa and reached past her shoulder to place a glass in front of her.

"No, thank you." Her baby girl's voice was strained.

"You don't want any champagne?" Josh was clearly confused. "You love the stuff. We practically finished off a magnum ourselves last New Year's Eve."

Melissa shook her head, her dark locks flying over her shoulder. "I'm sure. I'll just h-have—" She paused, pressing her fingertips to her mouth for a quick moment. "I'd prefer a cup of coffee. Decaf, please."

Oh, everything made sense now!

The tears, the exhaustion, the hand held protectively over her still flat belly, the refusal of alcohol. Her motherly intrusion might have been late in picking up on Melissa's distress, but the realization over what her baby was facing hit Diana like a thunderbolt coming from the sky.

Her heart didn't know whether to break for the certain pain Abby was facing over the end of her marriage or rejoice with the news that she was finally going to be a grandmother!

Her baby was having a baby!

Chapter Five
by Gina Wilkins

During the year he and Melissa Morgan had been together, Josh Wright thought he'd come to know her family fairly well, but there were still times when he felt like an outsider who couldn't quite catch on to the family rhythms. Tonight was one of those occasions.

The undercurrents of tension at the elegantly set dinner table were obvious enough, even to him.

Melissa had been acting oddly all evening. Abby and Greg kept exchanging significant looks, as though messages passed between them that no one else could hear. Even Melissa and Abby's mom, Diana, typically the life of any dinner party, was unnaturally subdued and introspective tonight. Only the family patriarch, Frank, seemed as steady and unruffled as ever, characteristically enjoying the time with his family without getting drawn in to their occasional, usually Diana-generated melodramas.

Josh didn't have a clue what was going on with any of them. Shouldn't he understand them better by now, considering he wanted so badly to be truly one of them soon?

He dipped his spoon into the dessert dish in front of him, scooping up a bite of fresh raspberries, an orange-liqueur-flavored mascarpone-cheese mixture and ladyfingers spread with what tasted like raspberry jam. "Abby, this dessert is amazing."

She smiled across the table at him. "Thank you. Mom and Dad had tiramisu the first night of their honeymoon, so I tried to recreate that nice memory."

"Ours wasn't flavored with orange and raspberry," Diana seemed compelled to point out. "We had a more traditional espresso-based tiramisu."

Abby's smile turned just a bit wry. "I found this recipe online and thought it sounded good. I wasn't trying to exactly reproduce what you had before, Mom."

"I think this one is even better," Frank interjected hastily, after swallowing a big bite of his dessert. "Who'd have thought thirty years later we'd be eating tiramisu made by our own little girl, eh, Diana?"

Everyone smiled—except Melissa, who was playing with her dessert without her usual enthusiasm for sweets. It bothered Josh that Melissa seemed to become more withdrawn and somber as the evening progressed. Though she had made a noticeable effort to participate in the dining table conversation, her eyes were darkened to almost jade and the few smiles she'd managed looked forced. As well as he knew her, as much as he loved her, he sensed when she was stressed or unhappy. For some reason, she seemed both tonight, and that was twisting him into knots.

Maybe Abby had been right when she'd warned him that his nervous anticipation was affecting Melissa, though he thought he'd done a better job of hiding it from her. Apparently, she knew him a bit too well, also.

Encouraged by the response to his compliment of the dessert, he thought he would try again to keep the conversation light and cheerful. Maybe Melissa would relax if everyone else did.

Mindful of the reason for this gathering—and because he was rather obsessed with love and marriage, anyway—he said, "Thirty years. That's a remarkable accomplishment these days. Not many couples are able to keep the fire alive for that long."

He couldn't imagine his passion for Melissa ever burning out, not in thirty years—or fifty, for that matter.

He felt her shift in her seat next to him and her spoon clicked against her dessert dish. He glanced sideways at her, but she was looking down at her dish, her glossy black hair falling forward to hide her face from him.

Frank, at least, seemed pleased with Josh's observation.

"That's it, exactly." Frank pointed his spoon in Josh's direction, almost dripping raspberry jam on the table-cloth. "Keeping the fire alive. Takes work, but it's worth it, right, hon?"

"Absolutely." Diana looked hard at Abby and Greg as she spoke. "All marriages go through challenging times, but with love and patience and mutual effort, the rewards will come."

Abby and Greg shared a startled look, but Frank spoke again before either of them could respond to what seemed like a sermon aimed directly at them. "I still remember the day I met her, just like it was yesterday."

That sounded like a story worth pursuing. Though everyone else had probably heard it many times, Josh encouraged Frank to continue. "I'd like to hear about it. How did you meet?"

Frank's smile was nostalgic, his eyes distant with the memories. "I was the best man in a college friend's wedding. Diana was the maid of honor. I had a flat tire on the way to the wedding rehearsal, so I was late arriving."

Diana shook her head. Though she still looked worried about something, she was paying attention to her husband's tale. "The bride was fit to be tied that it looked as though the best man wasn't going to show up for the rehearsal. She was a nervous wreck, even though her groom kept assuring her Frank could be counted on to be there."

Frank chuckled. "Anyway, the minute I arrived, all rumpled and dusty from changing the tire, I was rushed straight to a little room off the church sanctuary where the groom's party was gathered getting ready to enter on cue. I didn't have a chance to socialize or meet the other wedding party members before the rehearsal began. Five minutes after I dashed in, I was standing at the front of the church next to my friend Jim. And then the music began and the bridesmaids started their march in. Diana was the third bridesmaid to enter."

"Gretchen was first, Bridget next."

Ignoring the details Diana inserted, Frank continued, "She was wearing a green dress, the same color as her eyes. The minute she walked into the church, I felt my heart flop like a landed fish."

Diana laughed ruefully. "Well, that doesn't sound very romantic."

Frank patted her hand, still lost in his memories. "She stopped halfway down the aisle and informed the organist that she was playing much too slowly and that everyone in the audience would fall asleep before the whole wedding party reached the front of the church."

"Well, she was."

Frank chuckled and winked at Josh. "That was when I knew this was someone I had to meet."

Charmed by the story, Josh remembered the first moment he'd laid eyes on Melissa. He understood that "floppy fish" analogy all too well, though he'd compared his own heart to a runaway train. He could still recall how hard it had raced when Melissa had tossed back her dark hair and laughed up at him for the first time, her green eyes sparkling with humor and warmth. He'd actually wondered for a moment if she could hear it pounding against his chest.

"So it was love at first sight?"

Frank nodded decisively. "That it was."

"And when did you know she was 'the one' for you? That you wanted to marry her?"

"Probably right then. But certainly the next evening during the ceremony, after I'd spent a few hours getting to know Diana. When I found myself mentally saying 'I do' when the preacher asked 'Do you take this woman?' I knew I was hooked."

Josh sighed. This, he thought, was why he wanted to wait for the absolute perfect moment to propose to Melissa. Someday he hoped to tell a story that would make everyone who heard it say "Awww," the way he felt like doing now. "You're a lucky man, Frank. Not every guy is fortunate enough to find a woman he wants to spend the rest of his life with."

Three lucky men sat at this table tonight, he thought happily. Like Frank and Greg, he had found his perfect match.

Melissa dropped her spoon with a clatter and sprang to her feet. "I, uh— Excuse me," she muttered, her voice choked. "I'm not feeling well."

Before Josh or anyone else could ask her what was wrong, she dashed from the room. Concerned, he half rose from his seat, intending to follow her.

"What on earth is wrong with Melissa?" Frank asked in bewilderment.

Words burst from Diana as if she'd held them in as long as she was physically able. "Melissa is pregnant."

His knees turning to gelatin, Josh fell back into his chair with a thump.

After patting her face with a towel, Melissa looked in the bathroom mirror to make sure she'd removed all signs of her bout of tears. She was quite sure Abby would say she was overreacting and being overly dramatic—just like their mom, Abby would say with a shake of her auburn head—but Melissa couldn't help it. Every time she thought about her life without Josh in it tears welled up behind her eyes and it was all she could do to keep them from gushing out.

Abby had tried to convince her she was only imagining that Josh was trying to find a way to break up with her. As much as she wanted to believe her sister, Melissa was convinced her qualms were well-founded. She knew every expression that crossed Josh's handsome face. Every flicker of emotion that passed through his clear blue eyes. He had grown increasingly nervous and awkward around her during the past few days, when they had always been so close, so connected, so easy together before. Passion was only a part of their relationship—though certainly a major part. But the mental connection between them was even more special—or at least it had been.

She didn't know what had gone wrong. Everything had seemed so perfect until Josh's behavior had suddenly changed. But maybe the questions he had asked her dad tonight had been a clue. Maybe he had concluded that he didn't really want to spend the rest of his life with her. That only a few men were lucky enough to find "the one."

She had so hoped she was Josh's "one."

Feeling tears threaten again, she drew a deep breath and lifted her chin, ordering herself to reclaim her pride. She would survive losing Josh, she assured herself. Maybe.

Forcing herself to leave Abby's guest bathroom, she headed for the dining room, expecting to hear conversation and the clinking of silverware and china.

Instead what appeared to be stunned silence gripped the five people sitting at the table. Her gaze went instinctively to Josh, finding him staring back at her. His dark blond hair tumbled almost into his eyes, making him look oddly disheveled and perturbed. She realized suddenly that everyone else was gawking at her, too. Did she see sympathy on her father's face?

Before she could stop herself, she leaped to a stomach-wrenching conclusion. Had Josh told her family that he was breaking up with her? Is that why they were all looking at her like…well, like that?

"What?" she asked apprehensively.

"Why didn't you tell me?" Josh demanded.

It occurred to her that he sounded incongruously hurt, considering he was the one on the verge of breaking her heart. "Tell you what?"

"That you're pregnant."

"I'm—?" Her voice shot up into a squeak of surprise, unable to complete the sentence.

"Don't worry, darling, we'll all be here for you," Diana assured her, wiping her eyes with the corner of a napkin. "Just as we'll be here for you, Abby, after you and Greg split up. Although I sincerely hope you'll try to work everything out before you go your separate ways."

"Wait. What?" Greg's chair scraped against the floor as he spun to stare at his wife. "What is she talking about, Abby?"

Melissa felt as if she'd left a calm, orderly dinner party and returned only minutes later to sheer pandemonium.

"What on earth makes you think I'm pregnant?" she

asked Josh, unable to concentrate on her sister's sputtering at the moment.

He looked from her to her mom and back again, growing visibly more confused by the minute. "Your mother told us."

Her mother sighed and nodded. "I've overheard a few snippets of conversation today. Enough to put two and two together about what's going on with both my poor girls. You're giving up caffeine and you're feeling queasy and we've all noticed that you've been upset all evening."

"Mom, I don't know what you heard—" Abby began, but Melissa talked over her sister.

"You're completely off base, Mom," she said firmly, avoiding Josh's eyes until she was sure she could look at him without succumbing to those looming tears again. "I'm giving up caffeine because I think I've been drinking too much of it for my health. I'm not pregnant."

Regret swept through her with the words. Maybe she was being overly dramatic again, but the thought of never having a child with Josh almost sent her bolting for the bathroom with another bout of hot tears.

She risked a quick glance at him, but she couldn't quite read his expression. He sat silently in his chair, his expression completely inscrutable now. She assumed he was deeply relieved to find out she wasn't pregnant, but the relief wasn't evident on his face. Maybe he was thinking about what a close call he'd just escaped.

Her mom searched her face. "You're not?"

Melissa shook her head. "No. I'm not."

"Then why have you been so upset this evening?"

Rattled by this entire confrontation, she blurted, "I'm upset because Josh is breaking up with me."

Josh made a choked sound before pushing a hand through his hair in exasperation. "Why do you think I'm breaking up with you?"

"I just, um, put two and two together," she muttered, all too aware that she sounded as much like her mother as Abby always accused her.

"Well, then you need to work on your math skills," Josh shot back with a frustrated shake of his head. "I don't want to break up with you, Melissa. I want to ask you to marry me!"

Chapter Six
by Cindy Kirk

Bedlam followed Josh Wright's announcement that he planned to propose to Melissa Morgan. Everyone at the table started talking in loud excited voices, their hands gesturing wildly.

Family patriarch Frank Morgan had experience with chaotic situations. After all, he and his wife, Diana, had raised two girls. When things got out of hand, control had to be established. Because his silver referee whistle was in a drawer back home, Frank improvised.

Seconds later, a shrill noise split the air.

His family immediately stopped talking and all turned in his direction.

"Frank?" Shock blanketed Greg DeSena's face. Though he'd been married to Frank's oldest daughter,

Abby, for three years, this was a side to his father-in-law he'd obviously never seen.

Frank's youngest daughter, Melissa, slipped into her chair without being asked. She cast furtive glances at her boyfriend, Josh. It had been Josh's unexpected proclamation that he intended to propose to her that had thrown everyone into such a tizzy.

Even though Frank hadn't whistled a family meeting to order in years, his wife and daughters remembered what the blast of air meant.

"Darling." Diana spoke in a low tone, but loud enough for everyone at the table to hear clearly. "This is our anniversary dinner. Can't a family meeting wait until another time?"

Her green eyes looked like liquid jade in the candlelight. Even after thirty years, one look from her, one touch, was all it took to make Frank fall in love all over again.

If they were at their home—instead of at Greg and Abby's house—he'd grab her hand and they'd trip up the stairs, kissing and shedding clothes with every step. But he was the head of this warm, wonderful, sometimes crazy family and with the position came responsibility.

"I'm sorry, sweetheart. This can't wait." Frank shifted his gaze from his beautiful wife and settled it on the man who'd blurted out his intentions only moments before. "Josh."

His future son-in-law snapped to attention. "Sir."

Though Frank hadn't been a marine in a very long time, Josh's response showed he'd retained his commanding presence. "Sounds like there's something you want to ask my daughter."

"Frank, no. Not now," Diana protested. "Not like this."

"Mr. Morgan is right." Josh pushed back his chair and stood. "There *is* something I want to ask Melissa. From the misunderstanding tonight, it appears I've already waited too long."

Frank nodded approvingly and sat back in his chair. He liked a decisive man. Josh would be a good addition to the family.

"If you want to wait—" Diana began.

Before she could finish, Frank leaned over and did what he'd wanted to do all night. He kissed her.

"Let the man say his piece," he murmured against her lips.

Diana shuddered. Her breathing hitched but predictably she opened her mouth. So he kissed her again. This time deeper, longer, until her eyes lost their focus, until she relaxed against his shoulder with a happy sigh.

Josh held out his hand to Melissa. His heart pounded so hard against his ribs, he felt almost faint. But he was going to do it. Now. Finally.

With a tremulous smile, Melissa placed her slender fingers in his. The lines that had furrowed her pretty brow the past couple of weeks disappeared. His heart clenched as he realized he'd been to blame for her distress. Well, he wouldn't delay a second longer. He promptly dropped to one knee.

"Melissa," Josh began then stopped when his voice broke. He glanced around the table. All eyes were on him, but no one dared to speak. Abby and Greg offered encouraging smiles. His future in-laws nodded approvingly.

His girlfriend's eyes never left his face. The love he saw shining in the emerald depths gave him courage to continue.

"When I first saw you at the office Christmas party, I was struck by your beauty. It wasn't until we began dating that I realized you are as beautiful inside as out."

Melissa blinked back tears. Josh hoped they were tears of happiness.

"This past year I've fallen deeper and deeper in love with you. I can't imagine my life without you in it. I want your face to be the last I see at night and the first I see every morning. I want to have children with you. I want to grow old with you. I promise I'll do everything in my power to make you happy."

He was rambling. Speaking from the heart to be sure, but rambling. For a second Josh wished he had the speech he'd tinkered with over the past couple of months with him now, the one with the pretty words and poetic phrases. But it was across the room in his jacket pocket and too late to be of help now.

Josh slipped a small box from his pocket and snapped open the lid. The diamond he'd seen circled in her bride's magazine was nestled inside. The large stone caught the light and sparkled with an impressive brilliance. "I love you more than I thought it was possible to love someone."

He'd told himself he wasn't going to say another

word but surely a declaration of such magnitude couldn't be considered rambling.

Her lips curved upward and she expelled a happy sigh. "I love you, too."

Josh resisted the urge to jump to his feet and do a little home-plate dance. He reminded himself there would be plenty of time for celebration once the ring was on her finger.

With great care, Josh lifted the diamond from the black velvet. He was primed to slip it on when she pulled her hand back ever-so-slightly.

"Isn't there something you want to ask me?" Melissa whispered.

At first Josh couldn't figure out what she was referring to until he realized with sudden horror that he hadn't actually popped the question. Heat rose up his neck. Thankfully he was still on one knee. "Melissa, will you make me the happiest man in the world and marry me?"

The words came out in one breath and were a bit garbled, but she didn't appear to notice.

"Yes. Oh, yes."

Relief flooded him. He slid the ring in place with trembling fingers. "If you don't like it we can—"

"It's perfect. Absolutely perfect." Tears slipped down her cheeks.

He stood and pulled her close, kissing her soundly. "I wanted this to be special—"

"It is special." Melissa turned toward her family and smiled through happy tears. "I can't imagine anything better than having my family here to celebrate with us."

"This calls for a toast." Flashing a smile that was

almost as bright as his daughter's, Frank picked up the nearest bottle of champagne. He filled Diana's glass and then his own before passing the bottle around the table.

Greg filled his glass and those of Josh and Melissa's but Abby, his wife, covered her glass with her hand and shook her head.

Frank stood and raised his glass high. "To Josh and Melissa. May you be as happy together as Diana and I have been for the past thirty years."

Words of congratulations and the sound of clinking glasses filled the air.

Nestled in the crook of her future husband's arm, Melissa giggled. Normally her mom knew everything before everyone else. Not this time.

"You thought I was pregnant because I wanted decaf coffee," she said to her mother, "but yet you don't find it odd that Abby hasn't had a sip of alcohol tonight?"

For a woman like Diana who prided herself on being in the "know," the comment was tantamount to waving a red flag in front of a bull. She whirled and fixed her gaze on her firstborn, who stood with her head resting against her husband's shoulder. "Honey, is there something you and Greg want to tell us?"

Abby's cheeks pinked. She straightened and exchanged a look with her husband. He gave a slight nod. She took one breath. And then another. "Greg and I, well, we're…we're pregnant."

"A baby!" Diana shrieked and moved so suddenly she'd have upset her glass of champagne, if Frank hadn't grabbed it. "I can't believe it. Our two girls, all grown up. One getting married. One having a baby. This is truly a happy day."

Everyone seemed to agree as tears of joy flowed as freely as the champagne, accompanied by much back-slapping.

"Have you thought of any names?" Diana asked Abby and Greg then turned to Melissa and Josh. "Any idea on a wedding date?"

Suggestions on both came fast and furious until Abby realized the party had gotten off track. She pulled her sister aside. "The anniversary gift," she said in a low tone to Melissa. "We need to give them their gift."

"I'll get it." In a matter of seconds, Melissa returned, cradling the large basket in her arms.

Josh moved to her side, as if he couldn't bear to be far from his new fiancée. Greg stood behind his wife, his arms around her still slender waist.

"Mom and Dad," Melissa began. "You've shown us what love looks like."

"What it feels like," Abby added.

With a flourish, Melissa presented her parents with a basket overflowing with biscotti, gourmet cappuccino mix, and other items reminiscent of their honeymoon in Italy…along with assorted travel documents. "Congratulations on thirty years of marriage."

"And best wishes for thirty more," Abby and Melissa said in unison, with Josh and Greg chiming in.

"Oh, Frank, isn't this the best evening ever?" Diana's voice bubbled with excitement. "All this good news and gifts, too."

She exclaimed over every item in the basket but

grew silent when she got to the tickets, guidebooks and brochures. Diana glanced at her husband. He shrugged, looking equally puzzled.

"It's a trip," Abby explained.

Melissa smiled. "We've booked you on a four-star vacation to Italy, so you can recreate your honeymoon, only this time in comfort and style."

"Oh, my stars." Diana put a hand to her head. When she began to sway, her husband slipped a steadying arm around her shoulders.

"I think your mom has had a bit too much excitement for one day." Frank chuckled. "Or maybe a little too much of the vino."

"I've only had two glasses. Or was it three?" Instead of elbowing him in the side as he expected, she laughed and refocused on her children. "Regardless, thank you all for such wonderful, thoughtful presents."

Abby exchanged a relieved glance with Melissa. "We wanted to give you and Dad the perfect gift to celebrate your years of happiness together."

"You already have," Frank said, his voice thick with emotion.

He shifted his gaze from Abby and Greg to Melissa and Josh before letting it linger on his beautiful wife, Diana. A wedding in the spring. A grandbaby next summer. A wonderful woman to share his days and nights. Who could ask for more?

* * * * *

HEART & HOME

Heartwarming romances where love can
happen right when you least expect it.

 Harlequin®
SPECIAL EDITION®

COMING NEXT MONTH
AVAILABLE APRIL 24, 2012

#2185 FORTUNE'S UNEXPECTED GROOM
The Fortunes of Texas: Whirlwind Romance
Nancy Robards Thompson

#2186 A DOCTOR IN HIS HOUSE
McKinley Medics
Lilian Darcy

**#2187 HOLDING OUT FOR DOCTOR
PERFECT**
Men of Mercy Medical
Teresa Southwick

**#2188 COURTED BY THE TEXAS
MILLIONAIRE**
St. Valentine, Texas
Crystal Green

#2189 MATCHMAKING BY MOONLIGHT
Teresa Hill

#2190 THE SURPRISE OF HER LIFE
Helen R. Myers

You can find more information on upcoming Harlequin® titles,
free excerpts and more at www.HarlequinInsideRomance.com.

HSECNM0412

REQUEST YOUR FREE BOOKS!
2 FREE NOVELS PLUS 2 FREE GIFTS!

Harlequin

SPECIAL EDITION
Life, Love & Family

YES! Please send me 2 FREE Harlequin® Special Edition novels and my 2 FREE gifts (gifts are worth about $10). After receiving them, if I don't wish to receive any more books, I can return the shipping statement marked "cancel." If I don't cancel, I will receive 6 brand-new novels every month and be billed just $4.49 per book in the U.S. or $5.24 per book in Canada. That's a saving of at least 14% off the cover price! It's quite a bargain! Shipping and handling is just 50¢ per book in the U.S. and 75¢ per book in Canada.* I understand that accepting the 2 free books and gifts places me under no obligation to buy anything. I can always return a shipment and cancel at any time. Even if I never buy another book, the two free books and gifts are mine to keep forever.

235/335 HDN FEGF

Name	(PLEASE PRINT)	
Address		Apt. #
City	State/Prov.	Zip/Postal Code

Signature (if under 18, a parent or guardian must sign)

Mail to the **Reader Service:**
IN U.S.A.: P.O. Box 1867, Buffalo, NY 14240-1867
IN CANADA: P.O. Box 609, Fort Erie, Ontario L2A 5X3

Not valid for current subscribers to Harlequin Special Edition books.

Want to try two free books from another line?
Call 1-800-873-8635 or visit www.ReaderService.com.

* Terms and prices subject to change without notice. Prices do not include applicable taxes. Sales tax applicable in N.Y. Canadian residents will be charged applicable taxes. Offer not valid in Quebec. This offer is limited to one order per household. All orders subject to credit approval. Credit or debit balances in a customer's account(s) may be offset by any other outstanding balance owed by or to the customer. Please allow 4 to 6 weeks for delivery. Offer available while quantities last.

Your Privacy—The Reader Service is committed to protecting your privacy. Our Privacy Policy is available online at www.ReaderService.com or upon request from the Reader Service.

We make a portion of our mailing list available to reputable third parties that offer products we believe may interest you. If you prefer that we not exchange your name with third parties, or if you wish to clarify or modify your communication preferences, please visit us at www.ReaderService.com/consumerschoice or write to us at Reader Service Preference Service, P.O. Box 9062, Buffalo, NY 14269. Include your complete name and address.

HSE11B

*It's never too late for love
in Hope's Crossing...*

**A charming tale of romance and community
by *USA TODAY* bestselling author**

RaeAnne Thayne

"Romance, vivid characters and a wonderful story;
really, who could ask for more?"
—Debbie Macomber, #1 *New York Times* bestselling author,
on *Blackberry Summer*

Woodrose Mountain

Available now!

*After a bad decision—or two—Annie Mendes
is determined to succeed as a P.I. But her first assignment
could be her last, because one thing is clear: she's not cut
out to be a nanny. And Louisiana detective Nate Dufrene
seems to know there's more to her than meets the eye!*

*Read on for an exciting excerpt of the upcoming book
WATERS RUN DEEP by Liz Talley…*

THE SOUND OF A CAR behind her had Annie scooting off the
road and checking over her shoulder.

Nate Dufrene.

Her heart took on a galloping rhythm that had nothing to
do with exercise.

He slowed beside her. "Wanna ride?"

"I'm almost there. Besides, I wouldn't want to get your
seat sweaty."

His gaze traveled down her body before meeting her
eyes. Awareness ignited in her blood. "I don't mind."

Her mind screamed, *get your butt back to the house and
leave Nate alone.* Her libido, however, told her to take the
candy he offered and climb into his car like a naughty little
girl. Damn, it was hard to ignore candy like him.

"If you don't mind." She pulled open the door and
climbed inside.

The slight scent of citrus cologne, which suited him,
filled the car. She inhaled, sucking in cool air and Nate.
Both were good.

"You run often?" he asked.

"Three or four times a week."

"Oh, yeah? Maybe we can go for a run together."

Her body tightened unwillingly as thoughts of other
things they could do together flitted through her mind. She

shrugged as though his presence wasn't affecting her. Which it *so* was. Lord, what was wrong with her? *He* wasn't her assignment.

"Sure." No way—not if she wanted to keep her job. As he parked, she reached for the door handle, but his hand on her arm stopped her. His touch was warm, even on her heated flesh.

"What did you say you were before becoming a nanny?"

Alarm choked out the weird sexual energy that had been humming in her for the past few minutes. Maybe meeting him on the road wasn't as coincidental as it first seemed. "A real-estate agent."

Will Nate discover Annie's secret?
Find out in WATERS RUN DEEP by Liz Talley,
available May 2012 from Harlequin® Superromance®.

And be sure to look for the other two books
in Liz's THE BOYS OF BAYOU BRIDGE series,
available in July and September 2012.

HSREXP0412